Joseph's Last Resort

Sarah Lamb

A thank you to my proofreader, Brooke, and all of the lovely women who help ARC read to catch those typos I miss!

This book was not written by AI. Any typos are proudly (and embarrassingly!) my own human created ones!

Paperback ISBN: 978-1-960418-42-5
Large Print: ISBN: 978-1-960418-43-2

Contents

For those who wonder if they are good enough—you are.
I promise.

Chapter 1

1886, Oregon

Joseph McAllen's fist clenched the letter from the family lawyer so tightly, his hand ached. With a scowl, he looked down at it and then refolded the paper, shoving it back into the envelope like he'd done at least a hundred times since it arrived two weeks ago.

The page was filled with legal speak, all that fancy talk most people didn't understand, but the message was clear. *Be married by the time you are thirty-two, or the ranch goes to your cousin.* Joseph tucked the letter in his pocket and tried to slow his breathing.

Lose the ranch. Lose the hard work his father and his grandfather had spent decades building? Not to mention the three years he'd been working the land! How was it that he'd never known about this stipulation in order to keep it?

Joseph started to pace. Well, that wasn't quite right. He'd known that he had to get married to keep the place. Had always known. His grandfather had bought the land from a relative, who wanted to make sure it stayed in the family, hence the command that he must marry. If he didn't, it would go to the next closest relative. His cousin.

But he'd misremembered the age, thought it was thirty-five, not thirty-two. He'd thought there was plenty of time. Now, with less than a month until his birthday, he'd been forced to do something he never planned to do.

Get the first mail-order bride he could find.

He swallowed hard. The stage would be arriving at any moment. Bess was her name. If her advertisement, and then the letter and photograph that came soon after, was anything truthful, she had blonde curls and was small in stature, sweet natured, and eager to live out West.

Sounded pretty normal.

He hoped.

Problems could arise with mail-order marriages, though, and that was the part that had him feeling more than a little anxious. You just didn't know what you were getting until it might be too late. Sometimes, one party took advantage of the other. He'd read an article in the paper just last week about a man who'd lost a lot of money to a thieving bride who was actually part of a criminal gang.

Of course, in his mind, it was usually the woman who was most at risk. Moving all the way from everyone and everything she knew to become a stranger's wife?

Desperate. That's what those women must be, too, and since misery—desperation—loved company, perhaps they'd have that to bond over at first, until they discovered other similarities.

Surely, it would all work out. He was worried over nothing at all. Why, every man got nervous before his wedding day. Which would be pretty soon after they said howdy. Before sunset, anyway, in order to make sure it was all proper when she went back to the ranch.

"Where's that stage?" he muttered, checking the large clock on the stage station's pine wood wall. Every minute that ticked by made him more and more restless. Soon, he'd wear a ditch in the street if he didn't stop his pacing.

"Running late," the station manager agreed. "But it'll get here. Always does."

Joseph grunted and resumed his pacing. The whole situation upset him. It filled him with a restlessness he couldn't control since he got the letter two weeks ago.

He couldn't lose his ranch. Hester didn't deserve it. He'd run the place right into the ground! Hester was two years younger than him, and his father had run the bank. Now, Hester did. Or, rather, he pretended to. Everyone in town knew he didn't have a lick of sense about anything, which was why he had two bank managers, but if there was any chance of some sort of prestige, or wealth to be made, he was right there, sticking his grimy fingers into it.

Even if he lied, cheated, or stole to make it happen.

Hester only looked after himself and wanted a life of ease and comfort. So, what he'd want with a ranch that required a lot of hard work, and involved muck and animals, Joseph didn't know. Unless it was simply that he wanted it because Joseph had it, and he didn't.

"Thar she comes," the station manager hooted, slapping his hat onto his head. "Like she always does."

Joseph made sure his own hat was straight, tugged on the collar of his plaid shirt, and tried not to look like he'd been fretting, instead hoping the smile on his face was one of welcome, and not a grimace. He was sure he'd gotten a few dozen gray hairs as of late, wrinkles too. Would she spot them?

As the cloud of dust rolled across the town, he waited patiently as passengers alighted. Finally, a small woman with bright blue eyes, the complexion of a China doll, and blonde ringlets a little worse for the wear stepped out.

"Ma'am," Joseph said, stepping forward. "I'm Joseph. Are you Bess?"

"I...I am," she answered, turning her pert little nose up as she crinkled it. Her head turned slowly in each direction. "Well. This town isn't much."

He stiffened. What kind of greeting was that?

"It grows on a body," Joseph answered, trying to smile.

"I'm sure it does, along with the dirt, dust, and everything else." Bess looked him over.

Her critical gaze almost made him step back. Likely, he would have had he not been frozen in shock at her forwardness.

"You aren't what I expected," Bess said, pressing her lips together.

"No?" he asked, shoving his hands into his pockets to hide the anger filling him. This was the woman who was going to save his ranch? He was so desperate, he had to make it work, no matter the stinging insults she was casting. Perhaps she was just tired. Hungry. Biting words could come from a body like that. He had to watch his mouth.

"No. You aren't. I've had a lot of time to consider the situation on the drive here, and I don't think this will work."

"What?" Joseph's jaw dropped, then he pleaded, "You can't say that! You've just gotten here. We don't know each other yet." Joseph realized he was near begging, but didn't care. The situation was much too dire.

Bess turned back toward the stagecoach and started to climb inside. She didn't say a word.

"Wait! What are you doing?" Joseph called out, his voice filled with panic.

Finally, she paused, reached inside of her reticule, and dug around. Bess waved a scrap of paper in his direction. "I received a better offer the day after I got yours. They suggested I take a look, and if I didn't like what I saw, to go there instead."

She smirked. "I don't like what I see, and why would I want to be a rancher's wife when I could be something better? The wife of a hotel owner? I'll have servants, a cook, I'll live in a large suite of luxurious rooms, and I'll never have to work or smell filthy men or animals."

Joseph stared at her, dumbstruck, as the driver shrugged at him, and shut the stage door. In a whirlwind of dust once more, the stage roared past, and the reality of the situation sank in.

Not only was Joseph struggling to keep the ranch, but he'd just been rejected by the person he'd hoped would save it. Now what was he going to do?

Chapter 2

California

Ines Martin glanced around her bedroom. Her traveling trunk was packed, though she wasn't sure just how much she'd really need. Along with her clothing, she had packed three books, plus two for the small bag she'd carry with her, and hoped that would be enough. With any luck, she'd run across a small shop somewhere to get something new to read.

The plan was to chaperone her younger sister Lily to her future husband in Nevada. When their parents said they'd arranged a marriage to a steady, stable man via a matchmaker, Ines had been just as surprised as her sister.

Perhaps it was because Ines was older. She'd have thought they'd have wanted her to be married first, or helped her find someone too. But Lily had always been treated differently, as far back as Ines could remember. If there was something her sister wanted, she got it, and nothing stood in her way.

Not one to argue or want to cause problems, Ines had always just accepted what came her way. Though she'd tried to convince herself there was nothing wrong with that, that she was content with her life, it wasn't really the truth. The truth was that it was simply easier to step back and let her sister have her way. To blend into the background.

Shortly before their parents' shocking announcement, Lily had been talking about wanting to marry. However, Ines was sure it wasn't this man in Nevada her sister had wanted.

Still, Lily had agreed. And with a speed that made Ines just a little suspicious. How could she say anything, though? Her sister was the darling one. The pretty one. The one petted and doted on, so who would have believed Ines that Lily's sudden acceptance felt strange? Lily wasn't nearly as obedient as she pretended, but had managed to pull the proverbial wool over everyone's eyes.

Lily had all the luck.

Maybe some people wouldn't think so. After all, she was being shipped off to a husband she hadn't chosen. But Rosemary, a family friend who had found her sister's husband, assured them he was a good man, could provide well, and was sure to love Lily with all his heart.

And each time she'd heard that or thought about it, Ines's own heart ached.

Yes, she was jealous. Ines couldn't help it. Always overlooked because her vivacious, energetic, lovely sister drew every eye her way, Ines had just about given up any hope of ever finding a husband. There was a tiny spark of hope that with her sister gone, there might be a few gentleman callers for her, but Ines truly doubted that. If there was anyone interested in her in the least, he'd have made himself visible before now.

She'd be thirty later this year, and Ines had never had a romantic event in her life. No press of the lips to her hand or cheek or lips. No whispered words of affection. Not even a wink. There had been no love notes, no poems, no requests for a meeting.

Hot tears burned in her eyes, but Ines ignored them. Today—like every other day—was about her sister, and she just needed to get through it, like she always did.

A bit of travel would be nice, though. She'd never been to Nevada. And, who knew! Perhaps she'd find a man there interested in her. Why, one might even be on the train.

The idea made her smile. It likely would not happen, but hope didn't cost anything other than the risk of failure and tears, and, as Ines had experienced plenty of both, she'd hardly notice more.

"Girls, you need to hurry," their mother called. "The carriage is here."

Ines left her room and descended the stairs. "I'm ready."

"The driver will get your trunk," her mother said, motioning to the hired driver. She glanced around with a frown. "Where is your sister? Go get her."

Ines nodded, and hurried back up the stairs. When she got to her sister's door, she knocked. "Lily? Are you ready? The man is here to take us to the train station."

There was silence. Did that mean Lily was pouting? Ines hesitated, but knocked again. "We need to go," she said.

Her mother's footsteps sounded behind her. "What's taking so long?" she asked.

"She's not answering," Ines said.

"That girl," her mother muttered, and tried the doorknob. When it twisted open, Ines followed her mother inside of the room.

The corner bedroom, the best in the house. Gardens were out one side, and a large tree with branches she had often climbed with her sister when they were children.

"Lily?" her mother called. "Where are you? Stop this nonsense!"

Ines walked toward the window that was partially open, letting in the sweet scent of roses. Then, she stopped. On the bed was a single sheet of paper. As she read it, then read it again, Ines paled.

How could she? How could Lily do this to her? To her parents? Ines swallowed hard. "Mama," she said uncertainly. "I think you'd better read this."

Ines's mother took the offered letter and read it. Not a second later, she fainted.

Chapter 3

No wife, no options. That about summed up Joseph's life right now.

He dropped his head into his hands. He'd never felt so concerned in his existence. No, that was a lie. He wasn't concerned. He was terrified. Gutted. Devastated. He'd worked incredibly hard on the ranch since he was a boy, had always believed it would be his, and now...

How could the woman have done that? Just get here, take one look, and be gone again? And, even more alarming was the thought that crept into his mind, what would he do if that happened again? There wasn't a single woman in town he could marry. Not a single one, and it wasn't an exaggeration, unless one grew up or got widowed real quick.

The sound of footsteps shuffling over the dirt path to the barn had him glancing up. "You in here?" his foreman, Cal, asked.

"Sure am," Joseph said. Then, before he could stop himself, he bitterly added, "I was just looking around at all I have to lose."

Cal joined him, slowly staring through the wide barn doors out to the lush pastures where more cattle and horses than a man could easily count grazed contentedly. That wasn't even all there was. Besides the cattle and horses, there were hundreds of acres, the large house, an enormous orchard with eight kinds of fruit trees, a creek, a pasture of sheep, and a slew of hens near a garden that grew bigger each year.

"You haven't lost it yet," Cal said. "Not by a longshot."

"Need a woman to keep it," Joseph sighed. "And there's a severe drought of them around here."

Cal nodded slowly. "You aren't wrong on that," he told him. "What about..."

When the silence had stretched far longer than he'd have liked, Joseph asked, "What about what?"

"Well, I reckon you aren't wanting to risk another mail-order ad, seeing as you don't have much time. What you need is someone who knows a woman who is wanting to get married. And married fast. Didn't you tell me you had an aunt who did that sort of thing?"

"Aunt Rosemary?" Joseph pushed his hat up to rub at his head. "Well, yeah, but I'm not sure I'm wanting to write her."

"Why not? You're desperate, aren't you?"

"Well, I am," Joseph said, "but my aunt is...well, she's...and then she's..."

"That means you aren't desperate enough," Cal said, crossing his arms. "You've done waited until the last minute, boy. You got two choices. Let that lazy cousin of yours take over and run this place you and your daddy and your granddaddy worked so hard to build up—not to mention all of us men—or swallow your pride and put up with her whatever it is you can't seem to spit out, and ask her to find you a woman who won't get back on the stage the moment she arrives."

Joseph was quiet. Cal was right. He knew he was. That didn't mean he liked it, though. He gave himself a moment to think about what his foreman said. Then, he sighed deeply. "Fine. I'll go write her now."

Cal shook his head. "Can't nobody's aunt be that bad."

"It's not that she's bad," Joseph said. "It's that she's...and she's..."

"I'm likely never going to find out," Cal hooted, walking back to the fields, "because you ain't never going to spit it out!"

Joseph growled as he stomped back to the house. How could he? How was a man able to articulate Aunt

Rosemary to a body who had never met her? Their worlds were so different. Out in California, his aunt was a society woman. Teas and socials, fingers and nose in everyone's business.

She wrote every bit of it down too. The woman must have dozens of books by now containing every detail about everyone. He'd been there once as a child in her study, and picked up a book. He didn't know the person he'd been reading about, but when he'd read everything about them, from their family history to their current occupation, friends and connections, how they took tea, and then gotten to the bottom of the page, it read: *See book 11 for continuation.*

Aunt Rosemary was detailed. Exacting.

And...the more he thought about it, potentially just the right person to find the perfect woman for him. One who wouldn't leave. One who might be well suited to his life, perhaps help him. Be a friend. A marriage of convenience. At this point, he'd take anything. He wasn't looking for love. Love wasn't going to keep his ranch in his possession, not when there wasn't time to find it, anyway.

With another heavy sigh, though with a little more hope inside of him this time, Joseph got to work. After a few moments of writing, he studied the letter he'd written. Had he left out anything? He read it once more.

Dear Aunt Rosemary,

I hope that you are well. To my shame, I've not been in contact as much as I should have been, but I hope that you'll forgive me and help me. You know I inherited the family ranch. You also likely know that it will fall to the other half of the family if I'm not married by the time I'm thirty-two. I hadn't realized that. I thought I had until age thirty-five.

To be blunt, I need a wife, and I need your help to find one quickly. I am almost out of time. I'd found a mail-order advertisement and the woman sounded suitable, but when she arrived, she turned around and left again.

I'm desperate. I can't lose this ranch, the land that I love, and that my father, grandfather, myself, and so many other men have worked so hard to grow.

Please, can you help me? I have no other option but to entrust my future to your hands.

Your nephew,

Joseph

It would have to do. It was humiliating sending such a thing, but there was no other option. Putting the letter, along with all of his hope, into an envelope, Joseph saddled his mare and rode into town to mail the letter. He was fortunate to get there a minute before it was whisked away on the outgoing post. Now, all he had to do was wait.

And that's what he did. He didn't even know if Aunt Rosemary would help him. He rode to the post office every day, hoping for some notice that she'd gotten the letter, and that help, in the form of a marrying female, was on her way.

Joseph had just about given up. He'd heard nothing, and there wasn't much time left. Perhaps Hester would at least let him keep a little of the land. A few horses. Couple dozen cattle. Something.

"Anything?" he asked tiredly at the mail window.

"A few," the postmaster said, sliding a small stack to him.

Joseph flipped through the letters. Mostly mail for his men. But his heart started thumping when he saw his name written in a spidery handwriting he recognized, though it had been a long time since he'd seen it last.

Hardly able to hear anything for the pounding in his ears, Joseph tore it open. The letter was short, to the point. It simply read:

Help is on the way.

Chapter 4

There was a knock at the front door, and both Ines and her mother startled. After her mother had fainted, Ines and her father had helped her into a chair. The driver had been dismissed, and ever since the door closed behind him, Ines's mother had cried about how their reputation was ruined.

"Harumph," her father muttered as he scowled in the direction of the door. "Just what we need at a moment like this."

"Word has already gotten around," Ines's mother wailed.

"Perhaps not, Mother," Ines tried to assure her. However, she wasn't sure that was the truth.

Her father opened the front door, and tall, elegant Rosemary pushed her way in.

"I have heard the news," she said in that throaty voice of hers, while pausing in the doorway. Slowly, she shook her head. "You have my condolences, Charles. You too, Carlotta."

Her mother cried out, "Whatever will we do, Rosemary? Everyone will talk!"

"That they will," the older woman agreed. "But as for what you will do, I'm not sure. I suppose it depends on if you approve of the young man. However," she said, her eyes sweeping the room until they landed on Ines, "that is not why I am here."

"No?" Ines's father asked.

"I have come to see Ines," Rosemary said, her gaze sharp and her eyes piercing. "Carlotta, make us some tea."

It wasn't a request.

"Of...of course," Ines's mother said.

"Charles, this is women's talk," Rosemary said, raising a brow pointedly.

Her father gulped and rushed out of the room, not even bothering to look back. Her mother was right on his heels, promising to return in a moment.

Once her parents had left, Ines tried not to tremble. She didn't care for the sudden feeling she had about whatever was happening. Rosemary hadn't said a word, as she'd perched on the edge of a plush chair, placing her hands in her lap and staring at Ines consideringly.

Ines had tried to make small talk, to be a polite hostess while her mother wasn't there, but her tongue was stumbling so badly each time she tried, Rosemary had finally held up a hand.

"Stop," she ordered. "It's obvious you've been through a great shock this morning. Collect yourself, and our conversation will begin once your mother returns."

With a nod, Ines waited, finding her own chair and trying not to fidget. Her mother was back a short time later, looking flushed herself as she carried in a tea tray, and once they were all sitting there with tea before them, Rosemary spoke.

"Ines is not flighty, is she?"

"Not at all," her mother answered in surprise. She blinked a moment in confusion, then answered confidently, "She's sturdy as a rock."

"Not fearful around animals?" Rosemary raised her teacup and studied Ines overtop it.

When her mother looked at her for the answer, Ines shook her head. "No."

At least, as far as she knew. Her experience with animals had been somewhat limited, but how could one be fearful around a small creature? Most of them she'd met had been seeking scratches behind the ears or a saucer of cream. Nothing fearful at all, but instead, delightful and sweet.

"Good." Rosemary set her teacup down. "Ines. I have found someone for you to marry. We leave at once, if you agree."

Ines choked in a most unladylike way on her tea, and frantically dabbed at her face.

"Is that so?" her mother asked, the pained expression she'd worn not a half hour before suddenly gone, replaced by one of delight. Her mother's lips curled upward, but Ines felt goosebumps break out over her skin. She had no idea that her parents had been looking for someone for her to marry. Shouldn't they have told her?

Of course, she wanted that, eventually, but she also wanted love. To find someone who wanted her for herself. Not for convenience.

"Indeed, I have." Rosemary leaned forward slightly. "But the situation is such that it doesn't allow for much time at all to make your decision. You must trust me that he's suitable."

"Oh, we do! We do," Ines's mother said.

"Wait," Ines protested. "Don't I get any say? We know nothing about him. *I* know nothing about him. You would just send me away to a stranger?"

It was on the tip of her tongue to suggest that's why her sister had run away, since the man she'd been interested in had been denied her, and she'd been all but foisted upon a stranger. It was only her mother's stricken face, and the fact Ines didn't want to disappoint her that stopped her from speaking.

Her mother blinked rapidly. "Of course you do, dear. You get plenty of say in this entire thing! Why, I'd never choose your wedding dress. Unless it was unsuitable. Nor your travel suit. Though, I think you only have the one and there simply isn't time for another to be made, if you must go right away."

"I meant in the groom," Ines said dryly.

"Let me explain the situation," Rosemary said, commanding Ines's attention.

As the story unfolded, with what little the older woman knew from the letter, Ines felt sympathy fill her. She couldn't imagine having worked on a dream since childhood and to have it days away from being snatched from you. The older woman spoke highly of the family, of Joseph, and the times she'd met him.

She explained he was a man of integrity, devoted to his ranch, and the people who depended on him. He was also of means enough to provide for her, and keep her in comfort. While those were all very nice things, and Ines felt slightly better, the fact was he still was a stranger, and she didn't even know if he wanted her!

"My goodness," Ines's mother whispered, tears in her eyes. "That poor boy. He sounds so noble. Like something from one of those books you enjoy reading," she said to Ines.

Ines didn't answer. She wasn't sure anything that she could say, other than yes, would be heard.

"So you see," Rosemary said, her attention focused on Ines, "there isn't much time. I promise you, he is a good man. One who will take care of you. But perhaps, more importantly, if I may say so, beyond saving his inheritance, my nephew needs a woman like you, and you, my dear, need a man like him."

Ines was quiet.

This was a lot to take in. A long trip, a new state. A fresh start and a husband. Someone who lived in wide-open spaces, with perhaps a little more freedom than she had in this gossipy town. But, though she had Rosemary's assurances that Joseph was a good man, kind, and gentle, she'd also admitted it had been years since she'd seen him. What if the woman was wrong?

And how could she be so certain that Joseph needed her, beyond saving his ranch, and she needed him? No one had ever needed her. No one had ever wanted her, and the sting of that was, if Ines was to be truthful, more than stinging. It was devastating.

Always being passed up, always being overlooked. But, Joseph had felt the same, perhaps, hadn't he? If he'd not married yet and the very bride he'd chosen had rejected him on the spot?

Perhaps, even if love wouldn't be in her future, a mutual kindness and respect, friendship...that might exist. Many marriages started that way. Some even turned into love. Maybe hers would. If she said yes.

The idea made her less upset at her sister. Was it so wrong to wish for a chance at happiness? She could almost see Lily's letter she'd stumbled on. How she'd written, *I know you won't understand in the least, but I have an opportunity to be happy, and I want to take it.*

"It's a wonderful opportunity," Ines's mother gushed. "I cannot thank you enough for offering this to Ines. You have brought just the news we needed today."

Opportunity. There was that word again. Did that mean it was a sign? One to say yes?

"Of course I did," Rosemary said. She turned her sharp gaze to Ines. "But will you accept?"

Ines swallowed hard. "I don't feel as though I have a choice," she said quietly.

"You aren't being forced," Rosemary said, as she raised her hand to forestall Ines's mother. "It's simply that I know what's best. That doesn't, however, mean you have to accept the proposal." She slowly sipped from her tea and waited.

Ines nodded. No, she didn't have to accept. But if she didn't, not only might her life be very lonely, as she had no other option for marriage, but Joseph would likely lose his ranch. She wasn't sure that she could handle the guilt of that, not when she knew she could have prevented it.

It would be so far from home, though, and all the people and places she knew. That might not be a bad thing. But it would be different. If things didn't work out between her and Joseph, what would happen then?

Fear started to fill Ines. First in her stomach, then rising up to her chest and throat. She squeezed her hands together to hide their trembling.

"Ines," her mother said sharply. "Your answer."

"When would I leave?" Ines asked, bowing her head and saying what she knew her mother wanted her to say.

Rosemary consulted the small silver watch pinned on her lapel. "In an hour."

"An hour?" Ines gasped.

"Yes. But I assume you are already packed." The older woman shrugged.

"Oh dear! But a chaperone," her mother protested. "I can't arrange for one so quickly."

"I didn't mention?" Rosemary said, setting down her tea. "I'll be going with her. You and Charles can try to find a train to be there for the wedding."

Ines's mother nodded. Then she smiled at Ines. "I'm so happy for you, darling. I'm going to tell your father the wonderful news, but I'm afraid we won't be there. We simply must track down your sister. Prevent her from doing something foolish. Perhaps save our reputation before words gets out further, and while we still have a few shreds of dignity left. You'll write me every detail."

"Yes, Mother," Ines whispered.

Her mother flew out of the room, nearly overcome by excitement, but Ines stayed in her seat and twisted her fingers together in her lap. This morning, it was to be her sister married, now her. At least one thing was the same, a bit of travel. That, at least, she'd enjoy doing.

"Don't look so worried," Rosemary said. "I assure you, all will go well. And if it doesn't," she pressed her lips together as a fierce expression came over her face, "I'll make it."

Chapter 5

Help is on the way.

Joseph clung to that note from Aunt Rosemary, and tried to ignore the lingering concerns that would overwhelm him if he let them. It was in her hands now. There was simply nothing else he could do. Other than tend to the ranch and all the other work he had to do.

His damp shirt clung to him, and Joseph tugged at it, looking forward to getting back to the house and out of the sun so he could wash up and cool down. The weather had been brutal today, and with this heat, he had the suspicion that even when the sun went down, the temperatures wouldn't.

"Boss!"

He glanced up as Cal came riding up on his horse.

"That lawyer is here again," his foreman said, voice grim and face pinched.

"What? Why? I've another week and a few days," Joseph said. "What did he say he wanted?"

"Don't know. But I've come to tell you." Frank shrugged.

"Fine." Joseph sighed. "Might as well see what he wants."

"I'll send one of the boys out to finish checking the fences," Frank told him. "Then I will place the order for the wire we need at the south pasture tomorrow at the store."

Joseph nodded in answer, and rode back to the house. He tried not to look rushed or worried, but he was concerned that the apprehension was rolling off him like the beads of sweat on his forehead.

Not that it was much consolation, but the lawyer was looking as hot and as uncomfortable as Joseph felt, only he didn't have to work in a jacket, like the lawyer did.

"Afternoon," Joseph said, sitting in one of the chairs beneath the porch's shade. The lawyer had already sat, and half rose to greet him. They shook hands, and the lawyer sat on the edge of his chair.

"Hello, Joseph," the lawyer said. "I'm here about—"

"Let me guess, Mr. Altrose. You are here to find out if I am married or about to be." Joseph decided to get right to the point. He also didn't want to encourage the lawyer to stay, so he decided to potentially be rude, and not offer any refreshment.

"That's right." Mr. Altrose mopped at his damp brow with a handkerchief. "I heard tell that you sent away for a mail-order bride and she didn't even stay a full minute before she left."

His words stung, even though Joseph knew the man was speaking the truth. It was true she'd left quickly, but it was also true it might have been for the best. The two of them likely wouldn't have been suited to one another.

"You are running out of time, Joseph," the lawyer reminded him. "Your cousin is—"

"Not going to take this place and all the hard work that has gone into it," Joseph said firmly, crossing his corded arms over his chest. He kept his tone even, his face calm, polite even. It wasn't the lawyer's fault, he reminded himself. He was just doing his job.

"Then you have married?" Mr. Altrose asked, raising his eyebrows in surprise.

"Not yet, but she's on the way," Joseph said, hoping his words were the truth. When the lawyer continued to stare, waiting for him to say more, Joseph added, "Not that it's anyone's business but my own, but my aunt has found a lovely young woman who is eager to move West and live on a ranch."

Joseph also hoped those words weren't a lie. He didn't know for a fact that his aunt's brief message had meant she was sending a woman to him, but he sure had his fingers crossed. And, if she was, that the woman was accepting—even looking forward—to being on a ranch.

He didn't care about the "lovely" part, but a small part of him hoped even if she wasn't blessed with pleasing features, she'd at least have a pleasant way about her. Maybe she could even cook.

"Wonderful, wonderful," Mr. Altrose said. He stood. "You expect her soon?"

"Any day now," Joseph answered. He stood as well, and stuck out his hand. As he and the lawyer shook, he added, "I'm sure you'll be stopping back by, but just in case, I'll send word once we are wed."

"You do that," Mr. Altrose said. "I know I don't need to remind you what happens otherwise."

Joseph grimaced. "No. You don't."

His eyes followed the lawyer as he walked off of the porch, climbed up into his rented wagon, and set off toward the town. With a heavy sigh, Joseph turned, and then startled as his foreman appeared from the house.

"There you are," Cal said.

"I kept the conversation out here," Joseph said.

"Don't blame you. Something about that man gets my hackles up. Don't rightly trust him. The moment he thinks no one is looking, he drops that smile of his right quick." Cal spat in the dirt, then scowled in the direction of the wagon with the lawyer in it. "He also talks real fancy like sometimes. Don't like it. Don't like him."

Joseph laughed. "You and me both. Maybe it's just the situation. I'm sure Mr. Altrose is a fine man once a body gets to know him."

"Reckon maybe," Cal agreed, though he hesitated. "However, I've seen him hanging around your cousin's house a lot."

Now Joseph's eyes narrowed. "That so? You think that he's maybe been assisting my cousin in some way?"

"I don't know." The foreman frowned. "Just the same, maybe I'll ask around a little. With your permission."

Joseph nodded. "Might not be a bad idea. The fact that he knew I had a potential bride who didn't even stay a minute has me concerned. Someone must be telling him things. I hadn't told a soul about that woman, but for you and my aunt. She could have been anyone I was just passing the time with. Being polite to. No one was close enough to hear what she told me."

"I agree." Cal shook his head. "The ranch is too valuable for you to lose, especially to the likes of your cousin. It's been your sweat that's gone into it."

"Yours too," Joseph said quietly. "I won't ever forget that."

"You're a good man," Cal said. "A fair boss. You pay well. That's all I want in life."

Cal clapped Joseph on the shoulder and strode away. Joseph stared after him thoughtfully. That was all the foreman wanted? It was true, he did seem content. Joseph had been too, up until the lawyer told him he had to marry. Did that mean he wasn't the marrying kind?

What was he going to do when the time came he had a bride? He didn't know the first thing about how to treat women, let alone love one.

His dog wandered up, and Joseph reached down to scratch behind her ears. He'd found the small pup about two years ago, hiding in the barn right after a terrible rainstorm. The dog was a dark gray with a few specks, and Joseph had no idea the breed. She looked to be a little of everything. He'd called her Storm, and after asking around to see if she belonged to anyone, and fast becoming attached to the little one, Joseph was glad no one knew where she had come from or who might claim her.

The two became fast friends, and now Storm was as much a part of his day as the sunshine, hard work, or reading his Bible were.

"If Aunt Rosemary brings me a woman," Joseph told Storm, "I sure hope I know what to do. How to talk to her. Maybe be friends with her. Find her someone to make my days better, like you have."

The dog didn't answer, just lolled its tongue, and Joseph grinned. "Listen to me. I'm all assuming Aunt Rosemary will show up with one. But all I can do is hope that she does." He blew out a puff of worry. "Don't know what I'll do otherwise. I need a wife. One who won't leave me. One who will love the ranch as much as I do. One to help me."

The dog let out a little whine, and Joseph scratched at her ears again. As Storm's tail thumped against Joseph's boots, he whispered, "It's too much to ask a woman to be those things, especially when she hasn't had a chance to see me or the ranch first. But that's what I'm holding onto hope for. That, and maybe one day, even a little bit of love."

But as soon as he said those words, Joseph felt that painful squeeze of his heart. His mail-order bride had looked at him with such disdain, he'd felt downright unwanted. If that was the case, who would ever love him?

Chapter 6

"Back straight, and don't gape out the window!"

Ines quickly straightened from where she'd been leaning to get a better look at the countryside as it sped past them. The train was, as her traveling companion had put it, serviceable at best.

"But one cannot help the circumstances," the older woman had mumbled a few times. "Comfort must be sacrificed for speed."

Ines focused on a field of wildflowers, their purples and reds dotted with a few small clusters of yellow and white. She wondered what kind they were, as she'd never seen them before, but they quickly passed by before she could ask, and mountains in the distance, capped with snow, even though it was late summer, caught her interest instead.

The scenery was breathtaking, and it was hard not to gape, as Rosemary—Aunt Rosemary, as she'd told Ines to call her—reminded. She'd wondered if perhaps she'd tire of looking beyond the glass window, but so far, she hadn't. Every mile brought something to capture her attention.

While Ines was enjoying seeing these new sights, there was still a lot of worry filling her. What would Joseph be like? Would they get along? Would he be glad to see her or disappointed if she wasn't at all what he expected or hoped for?

And what did he expect or hope for? A woman to marry, that much was certain. But anything else? Did he want someone pretty? Clever? She wasn't sure those things were her. Ines was just...herself. Ordinary.

So far, that hadn't gotten her anyone interested in her. It was likely this time would be the same. Only, he'd be stuck with her. How would he react?

Those were only a few of the questions she had. There were a good number of other ones about the new place where she'd be living. She'd never been on a ranch before. What would that be like? Would she need to work with the animals? Cook for a horde of men?

It made sense now, Aunt Rosemary's question about whether animals frightened her. Ines almost laughed at the idea she'd thought the woman meant small, sweet, and fuzzy things. Not large and smelly livestock!

"There's no need to worry," Aunt Rosemary said, peering at Ines overtop of the book she held in her hand.

"Yes, ma'am," Ines whispered, looking down into her lap where her own book sat.

"Aunt Rosemary," the older woman corrected again. "We are about to be related." Her lips pursed just then. "Though, perhaps that's not a good thing, considering your sister's recent antics."

Ines's heart sank into her stomach. "I will do my best not to disappoint you. I wish I had known what she was planning. Over and over, I keep wondering if somehow I could have stopped her."

Aunt Rosemary shook her head. "You can't, not a person like that. It isn't your fault, dear, and I'm looking forward to having *you* in the family. You are a fine young woman, and will be just what Joseph needs."

"Are you sure?" Ines asked, twisting her fingers. "I know that you've said that, but I don't know anything about being a rancher's wife."

"Maybe not, but you are a clever girl, and you'll learn whatever it is you need to know quickly." Aunt Rosemary fluttered her hand around dismissively and tsked. "I'm sure he has help there, so it will likely simply be overseeing things."

Nodding, Ines tried to smile. Perhaps the other woman was correct. She hoped so, at any rate. "Do you think...do you think it will be a good marriage?" Ines asked quietly.

"Between your sister and that rapscallion she ran away with?" Aunt Rosemary asked. Her throaty, "I doubt it!" quickly followed.

Ines swallowed hard. "No, I meant for me and Joseph."

"Ahhh." Aunt Rosemary nodded. "I do. In time. All things need time to mature and blossom, from gardens to romances."

"What about you?" Ines asked. "Did your marriage take time?"

Aunt Rosemary arched a brow. "We are not talking about me," she said, and then made the smallest of gestures with her hand. "And how many times must I remind you? You might be on your way to become a rancher's wife, but you are soon to be part of my family, and are expected to have impeccable manners."

Ines straightened her back once more and nodded. She thought perhaps she'd best stop talking, as she didn't want to be scolded anymore.

The next half hour was spent in silence, when Aunt Rosemary suddenly said, "Somewhere around here, my niece Rose and her husband—one I matched her with—have a lovely place. Horses are what the two of them do. Something about teaching others to be wranglers, and the proper care of the animals. I don't know the full details, but it's added to their already considerable income," she said approvingly.

As she glanced at Ines, her face softened for just a moment as she added, "And the two are quite in love. Remind me to tell you their story sometime. And that of Millie and Winston." She smiled in satisfaction. "Yet another successful match. In fact, that wasn't the only one made around that time."

Knowing that there had been love matches made did make Ines feel a little better, and that terrible tightness she'd been feeling in her chest eased slightly.

"I appreciate you traveling with me," Ines said. "I've never gone anywhere, really, and this is the furthest I've been from home."

"I don't mind traveling," Aunt Rosemary said, letting her eyes roam around the train's car, "but I do prefer it in a bit more comfort. However, speed was necessary." A look of concern came over her face. "I just hope that Joseph still has the ranch and we aren't too late. It appears that my nephew isn't good at remembering dates. It is a concern of mine he's gotten this one mistaken as well."

"I hope we are too," Ines said. "I wouldn't want to have come all this way for nothing."

Sharp eyes fell on her. "It's not for nothing. You are going to be married."

Ines almost sensed an unspoken *like it or not*, but the truth was, though she was nervous, she was also just a tiny bit excited. She'd never thought that she'd have the opportunity to be married, run her own house, perhaps have a family. Whatever happened, she'd make the best of it. There really was nothing else to do.

The train began to slow, and Aunt Rosemary stowed her book into her handbag. "This will be our stop," she said. "Make ready. I am most eager to get off of this thing."

Ines nodded, and the moment the train stopped, they followed the small stream of people exiting.

"Now the terrible part," Aunt Rosemary said. "We have to take the stage." She said the words as though the mode of transportation was ghastly. "Quickly, quickly. It departs soon."

Ines followed, watching as Aunt Rosemary made sure their luggage was tied carefully to the stagecoach. They squeezed in, and for the next two hours, Ines bounced and jolted, winced, and covered her nose from the dust.

When the stage driver called their stop, she all but fell out of the stagecoach in relief. No wonder Aunt Rosemary had been so critical. Ines thought she'd have rather walked than ride in such a thing again.

Ines pointed out their trunks and bags, supervising as the stage driver removed them. Then, she and Aunt Rosemary stood on a wooden platform, glancing around. They were here. But, now what? Ines didn't know what to expect, or even what Joseph looked like. When she'd asked, his aunt had told her that appearances were like apples. One never knew what they'd get until they bit into it.

While Ines didn't have any intention of biting anyone, she understood. More than once, she'd had her mouth water over a juicy looking apple, only to bite in and find it was so sour she'd puckered.

Still, it would be nice to at least know who she was supposed to be looking for. Men, women, and couples of all ages went this way and that through the town. It was impossible to know which man might be Joseph. So, she let her eyes wander over the small buildings instead.

There was a dressmaker, a barber, a good-sized general goods store, a diner, a hotel, and—

Aunt Rosemary let out a loud harumph, and strode over to the ticket window. "Young man," she said, addressing the man behind the window, who was looking at her apprehensively. "I am looking for my nephew. Joseph McAllen. I had expected him here with transportation to his ranch. He has not come. I need you to arrange some for me."

"Oh, well, that's not really—"

"I'll be right over here," Aunt Rosemary said, indicating a bench. "And I'm in quite a hurry. Thank you."

She quickly moved to the bench and sat down, lips pressed together in irritation. Ines sat next to her, a little unsure whether they'd get the help they needed, but about twenty minutes later, a wagon hitched with two horses stopped nearby.

"You heading to the McAllen ranch?" the driver asked.

"We are," Aunt Rosemary said. She indicated to their bags. "If you'd be so kind? I'll pay you upon arrival."

The man nodded, and a short time later, they were heading away from town. Ines kept her handkerchief pressed against her nose and mouth, in a perhaps futile effort to decrease the dust getting into her face.

"Sorry 'bout that," the driver apologized. "Ain't been no rain fer a spell."

A single curt nod was Aunt Rosemary's only reply, but Ines offered, "It's quite fine," and then regretted it instantly, as her mouth filled with grit.

They jolted along, and just when Ines was sure neither her back nor her backside could take another bump, the driver called out, "We're almost there."

"If he weren't family," Aunt Rosemary murmured throatily from behind her handkerchief.

Before Ines could ask any questions, they rose over a hill, and the ranch spread before them. A large house, a barn, several outbuildings, and men and animals of several types everywhere. Ines's eyes widened, and grew even bigger as the wagon stopped in front of the house, alongside two men.

The younger of the two glanced first at her, then at her traveling companion. At first his expression was wary, then he squinted and asked, "Aunt Rosemary? Is that you?"

Chapter 7

"I have arrived," Aunt Rosemary said, looking Joseph up and down. She let him help her from the wagon.

"I...if I'd known you were coming today, I'd have sent a wagon," he apologized. He stole a glance at his aunt's traveling companion, wondering if she'd come to marry him. As his aunt hadn't introduced her yet, he didn't want to assume. Or say something and make a fool of himself. Especially if it wasn't so.

"Dear boy, you asked for my help. I told you it was on the way. The proper thing would have been to have someone waiting there every moment until I arrived." Aunt Rosemary gave him a sharp glance. "But I suppose out here, where there isn't proper civilization, you don't know these things."

"Forgive me," Joseph said, though he didn't feel the least bit apologetic. His eyes met the young woman's, and he offered, "Hello."

The woman's cheeks reddened, and she glanced first at his aunt, and then down at her boots. "Hello."

So she was here to marry him. Joseph swallowed. The moment had come. The woman was lovely, even if she seemed extremely shy. Considering the circumstances, however, he sure didn't blame her.

"Joseph, this is Ines Martin," Aunt Rosemary said, making introductions. "I think you will find she is just what you need, and I have brought her to be your wife."

"Praise be," Cal said. "We've been waiting for a woman to come in and rescue him."

"Well," Aunt Rosemary said. "Two have arrived. And who are you?"

"This is Cal, my foreman and good friend," Joseph explained quickly.

"It's good to meet you," Ines said, "both of you. You've a much larger ranch than I could have imagined."

"I can show you the house now. Cal, can you get their bags brought in?" Joseph asked.

"Sure can," Cal said, while his aunt sniffed loudly.

"Do be careful. Don't drop them," she said. "I'd never be able to find replacements out here." She opened her purse and paid the driver, then turned to the house, picking her way carefully up the porch steps.

As they walked inside, Aunt Rosemary asked, "Where is your housekeeper? I'd like to make her acquaintance and let her know my preferences."

"I don't have one," Joseph said. "I do my own cooking and cleaning."

Ines brought her hands to her lips to hide her smile at Aunt Rosemary's sudden expression of horror. Joseph didn't bother hiding his grin. The older woman had stopped, nearly sagged against the wall, and closed her eyes, slowly shaking her head.

"Aunt Rosemary?" Joseph asked finally. "Are you...all right?"

"What have I brought you to, Ines?" the older woman gasped. "No housekeeper. And a home this large? What will people say? What will your mother think? If word gets around..."

"Never mind," Ines said quickly. "We didn't have one at home, and I managed quite well. I expect I will do the same here."

Aunt Rosemary patted her arm. "You are a brave soul. I knew I was right to choose you. Joseph, I must rest after that horrible journey. We had to sacrifice comfort for speed, and I am about to collapse. Please, show me to my room."

"Ah, it will be that one right there," Joseph said, pointing to a door. "Ines, you can have the one next to that." He hesitated. "I need to get back outside. Will you be all right for a little while?"

"We will have to be," his aunt said with a shudder. "Though, I just hope I survive out here. It's more...rugged than I thought it would be. No wonder you can't find a bride. Are there even women in this forsaken area?"

Joseph gritted his teeth, and glanced at Ines. She hadn't said much since she'd gotten here, and he wondered what her opinion of the situation was. A flash of heat shot through him. Did she even want to be here? Was she just a means to an end, for her family, for his aunt, for him? He knew women didn't always get a lot of say in their future. Was that the case for her? And why she was so quiet? Maybe she wasn't shy, but scared. If things were reversed, he might be, too. Still, if this was going to be her home, and him her husband, he didn't understand why she wasn't speaking just a little more.

"Thank you," Ines said quietly just then. Her voice was sweet, even if she still didn't quite meet his eyes. "You've a lovely home, and I'm sure we will be most comfortable."

"You're welcome," Joseph said, feeling awkward. He shouldn't be so judgmental. That was Aunt Rosemary's department, not his. He was just tired of the whole mess and eager for it to be done with. "Help yourselves to anything you see. I've got to get back to work." He walked to the door, then turned, this time letting his gaze linger on the woman he was to marry. The woman who was to save his ranch. He hoped he'd get a chance to know her, at least a little bit, before they wed.

Of average height, Ines had dark brown hair that curled softly, he could tell. She had it pinned into a braid wrapped around her head, but a few tendrils had escaped. He wondered how long it was when it was loose. Her eyes were clear, a warm honey color, and she looked quick to laugh. He thought he might like that, and wondered how she'd enjoyed the journey with his aunt and her fussy ways. The thought made him smirk.

Maybe once she'd relaxed, as their journey had likely been long and exhausting, he'd see a little more personality from her. Perhaps his aunt was just overbearing, and that's why she was so quiet. Joseph wasn't sure, but he hoped she'd talk more. He liked her voice and wanted to hear more of it.

Ines turned, seeming to sense him looking at her, and when their eyes met, blushed under his scrutiny. A current flooded Joseph, striking his stomach, traveling to his heart where it beat wildly. Had Ines felt something? Her eyes had widened, and her lips parted slightly in surprise. So maybe she had.

Just what did that mean? He hadn't ever felt such a thing with anyone else. Maybe that was a good sign.

Joseph hurriedly turned, unwilling to linger any longer over what that moment might have been, and went outside. His arms felt tingly, and he balled his hands into fists and took slow breaths, forcing himself to calm down.

Not for the first time did the seriousness of the situation weigh on him. And, despite Ines's quiet assurance she could run the home without a housekeeper, when Joseph looked at her, sure, he saw an attractive woman, one he could easily and happily be around, but he also saw someone who didn't look confident in being there.

Could he blame her? She'd likely come from the city. And quite possibly not willingly. After all, not too many women came out this way on a whim. No, they had to have a reason for it. What was hers? Or did she even have one, since his aunt had brought her? Maybe it was simply she couldn't find a husband and wanted one.

As for her comfort…His aunt brought up a good point. While she might not have had a housekeeper, Ines may have had a cook or some maids. She was likely used to a softer life. One of luxury and fine entertainment. Not the simple things folks around here enjoyed, like barn raisings and sunsets and picnics on Sundays.

He might not know a lot about women's clothing, but he was able to tell, just from looking at her, that her clothes and likely her shoes were more suited for having tea or shopping than doing chores. Her skin was so fair, he felt sure her hands were the same, and had never done a day's work in her life. That just wasn't boding well for him. Or her.

Joseph blew out a breath. He should have known his aunt would find him a woman to marry. After all, that's what he'd asked for. But maybe he should have been specific on what he wanted—needed. A girl like Ines...she was too lovely and delicate looking to be able to survive out here. It wasn't the best way to start a marriage. It wouldn't be long—maybe even at the first snake sighting—before she was trying to get back to where she'd come from.

He groaned then, as he trudged toward the barn. The situation was hopeless. It was. Give her a day or two, and she'd be gone, just like the other woman. The only thing he could do was not let himself get attached, no matter he was already feeling a tug toward her. She'd leave him, a girl like that. Even if she stayed long enough to help him keep the ranch, that didn't mean she'd stay forever. Why would she? There wasn't anything here for her. And if she did leave, was there something in the will saying that he'd still lose the ranch? He'd have to reread it.

He stopped, turning back to look at the house and the pastures beyond. Joseph half wondered if losing the ranch and starting over would be better than being with a woman who might one day resent him for her role in this.

Another ranch could always be bought. Built up. He was no stranger to work. As a matter of fact, most days it felt like he was married to the ranch. His father used to warn him to take a little time, settle down, and enjoy life before he was too old to do it, but Joseph had always laughed. Even now, he didn't see wisdom in those words. Work would always be around.

Would Ines be understanding of that?

He hadn't seen it yet, but he could easily imagine her eyes filled with pain and hurt and sorrow being here, away from all she knew and loved, and him always fixing or overseeing something on the ranch.

And he'd never admit it to anyone, but Joseph knew the moment he saw that, his own heart could be crushed, because something was drawing him toward Ines.

And it scared him.

Chapter 8

It was a rare moment alone since she'd left her home in California, and Ines took the opportunity to close her eyes, breathe in the clear, cool air deeply, and then gaze at the enormous snow-covered mountains off in the distance.

It was curious to her how, even though it was already warming up that day, patches of snow still decorated the mountain tops. Had they been there since they fell? She wanted to ask Joseph, but felt a little shy still at the idea of talking to him.

It was beautiful. Oregon was breathtaking. From the wide-open spaces to the tiny wildflowers, the grasses, and the occasional tall tree she wasn't familiar with and, of course, the mountains. And this...this wondrous place, it could be her home.

Though they'd just arrived the afternoon before, it had been a whirlwind. Once Joseph had pointed them to their rooms, Aunt Rosemary had gone to rest for a while. Ines had changed her dress and washed up, but feeling restless and desiring to make herself useful, had soon found herself in the kitchen where she started to make an apple cake, and seeing that it grew later in the day, made biscuits and a hearty vegetable stew.

Her initial fears that Joseph didn't really mean for her to make herself at home had vanished as soon as he walked in with an appreciative sniff. "Smells good," he told her. "Thank you for making dinner."

Aunt Rosemary had swept in, and dinner was spent with those small questions people asked, trying to get to know each other a little better. Joseph had explained in better detail about the legal need to be married to keep the ranch, and had answered his aunt's questions about what would become of the place otherwise.

They'd gone to bed soon afterward. Ines read for an hour, wanting to finish the book she'd been unable to read on the train. She hadn't been sure Aunt Rosemary would approve of a fiction title, and that's all she happened to have with her.

After the heroine's happy ending, and a swoony kiss, Ines had sighed happily, closed the book, and slept soundly, even though she'd been fearful she wouldn't be able to, what with being in a new place and having so many questions.

Joseph had risen before them, and Ines felt guilty she hadn't had breakfast waiting for him. When she saw him next, she'd ask what time she should wake. In the meantime, she'd made some tea and toast for Aunt Rosemary and taken it to her, then slipped out here for a few moments alone.

It wasn't that being inside and with Aunt Rosemary was terrible, no. After all, the woman was her chaperone. It was just that Ines had hardly had time to think, except for when she was in her bed last night, and her weary body's needs had overcome those of her mind.

After seeing Joseph, and stealing a few glances at him over the table last night, there were more questions added to all those she'd arrived with. She kept wondering why he hadn't married sooner. Surely, any woman would be thrilled to be with a man like him. He was financially well off, and more than just a little handsome. At one point, he and his aunt had been reminiscing over something, and the way he'd laughed made his face light up, his eyes crinkle at the corners, and for some reason that she just couldn't explain, Ines loved his expression.

However, she'd had so little experience and interaction with men, she couldn't tell at all if he liked her. So far, he hadn't sought her out alone, and his conversations were polite, but not personal. Perhaps he wasn't really wanting anyone more than someone to save his ranch. But, she'd known that might be a possibility.

Movement around the side of the porch caught her eye, drawing her from the dark thoughts that were about to swim through her, and Ines looked in surprise as a dog walked toward her, then sat before her, patiently waiting. "Ah, hello," Ines said uncertainly, reaching out to let it sniff her fingers.

The dog butted its head against her hand and swished its tail. With a smile, Ines scratched behind its ears. "Like that, boy?"

"Girl, actually," a voice said, and Ines startled as Joseph came around the corner. "Sorry, I didn't mean to scare you," he said as he joined them. The dog ran right over to him. "This is Storm. Found her as a pup, and she's been with me ever since."

"Good to meet you, Storm," Ines said, smiling at the dog. She shyly added, "I apologize for not having breakfast ready for you. What time should I get up tomorrow?"

"Oh." Joseph blinked. "I hadn't even noticed. I usually breakfast with the men in the bunkhouse. You get up whenever you want. Most of the time, my midday meal is simple, and often carried with me. Bread, jerky, cheese, fruit. That sort of thing. I did welcome that hearty supper." He grinned. "You're a fine cook."

"Thank you," Ines said, glad he'd said so. "I'll be sure to cook every night. And you'll tell me if you want me to do the other meals?"

"I will," Joseph promised. "You might have to, while my aunt is here." He hesitated. "Do you...do you know how long she's staying?"

"She's my chaperone," Ines said, "so I think at least until we are married."

"I'm sorry," Joseph said, shaking his head.

Ines felt her pulse race. She swallowed. This was it. She knew it. "Sorry? For...being married?"

"No, not that," he quickly assured her. "Sorry for you having to have Aunt Rosemary around so long. She can be...well, she can be..."

He didn't finish, but Ines laughed, feeling relieved. "It's quite all right. I like Aunt Rosemary, actually. She can be demanding, but she also has a way of making you feel cared for. My posture may never be up to her standards, but I do find her a lovely woman."

"I just hope this place isn't too much for her." Joseph grimaced and waved his hand around, to gesture to the house and animals grazing. "Or for you. I know it's a far cry from the city, where both of you are from. There aren't fancy parties, and teas, and social events of the likes you both are used to."

Ines wasn't sure where he'd come to that assumption about her, and had opened her mouth to tell Joseph she didn't need those things, and had rarely enjoyed them, when the front door opened, and Aunt Rosemary strode forth, hands on her hips. "There you are! I can't find the sugar, Ines."

"It's in a small bowl on the table," Ines said. "Let me go get that for you."

"No need, I drank a pauper's tea," Aunt Rosemary said, almost proudly, and tossed her head. "I, too, can do my part to make scant supplies last longer out here in the wilderness."

"My ranch isn't exactly in the wilderness," Joseph said, "and you use as much sugar as you want. Tea too. I can get as much as you need from the general store. I'm not a pauper."

"Yet," his aunt corrected. "Now, let's talk marriage."

Ines was glad she wasn't holding the mug of tea she'd almost brought out with her, for she was sure to have choked on it over the blunt way the older woman spoke, but the topic did need to be decided upon.

"Ah, yes." Joseph looked uncomfortable. "I've got ten days before they'll take the ranch."

"Then you'll be married in nine," Aunt Rosemary declared. "In case you've miscounted again. That's not a lot of time, but it's what must be done."

She fixed Ines with a critical eye. "Have you anything suitable to wear, or must we go in search of something appropriate in this barren wasteland?"

"I...I don't know," Ines said. "I have dresses. But I don't know if they'll be up to your standards."

"My standards? *My* standards?" Aunt Rosemary pressed her lips together. "My dear," she began, rather throatily, as she held a hand to her chest, "this is to be your *wedding day*. You only get one. Usually. I'd think you'd want to look your best."

"Yes, ma'am," Ines apologized. "I only meant—"

Aunt Rosemary just shook her head. "And you, Joseph. I expect you at the church in something nice. Not that." She waved her hand up and down the length of him to indicate his work clothes.

"Yes, ma'am," Joseph said. "I promise."

His aunt nodded, then she clapped once. "Good. Now, the next matter at hand. The two of you."

"What about us?" Ines asked.

"You need to get to know each other a little better. I suggest a walk, within my eyesight. Perhaps a picnic. After your cousin Rose, and what she did the second my back was turned..." Aunt Rosemary's voice faltered, then she fiercely said, "There will be no shenanigans while I am about."

"I wouldn't dream of it," Joseph said. He stepped closer to Ines, and she felt a strange combination of both pleasure and bashfulness as he took her hand in his larger one. "I'll be on my best behavior."

"If a picnic is agreeable," Ines said, "I could put one together for us."

"I'd really like to show you around the ranch," Joseph said, rubbing at his jaw, "but Aunt Rosemary, I wonder if that might be too much for you. I usually go on horseback. The wagon can't go everywhere."

Aunt Rosemary winced. "Yes, it might be too much, dear. My aging bones, you know. I am still not yet recovered from the ride here. I suppose...if you promise to not do anything that would risk anyone's reputation, perhaps you two young people could go about on your own this afternoon. After all, you will be married soon."

"I promise," Ines said. "You've nothing to worry about. I'm-I'm not Lily."

Aunt Rosemary's face softened. "I know, dear."

"And I'm not Rose," Joseph said. He laughed. "I'm the obedient one in the family."

"I need to hear more about her," Ines said. "She sounds quite..."

"Feisty." Joseph grinned. "She's incredible."

"Willful," his aunt sniffed. "But she'll do. A good head on her shoulders."

"Why don't you go make us something to eat?" Joseph asked Ines. "I'll get two horses, and we'll head out." He started toward the barn. "You can ride, can't you?"

"A little," Ines said. "But not much."

"Not a problem," Joseph said.

Ines hurried into the house, where she searched until she found a large basket with a handle. She filled it with bread, a knife to cut it, a wedge of cheese, some leftover slices of cake, and a jar of strawberries she'd picked earlier that morning.

"Better take something to drink," Aunt Rosemary said. "It might be a dusty, dry ride."

With a nod, Ines packed a few jars of water, and then froze. She was about to be all alone with Joseph for the first time. The idea should have been exciting. After all, they were going to be married, but she felt scared. What if he didn't like her? She hadn't been able to tell. What if she did something foolish or stupid that made him dislike her?

The worry came to her mind again, how she didn't have much experience to draw on with men. How was she to know what to do? He always seemed hesitant of her. Was it simply because she came from the city, or was it something more?

"Be yourself," Aunt Rosemary said quietly, as if she could read Ines's mind. "That's all you have to be."

"But what if that's not enough?" Ines whispered fearfully.

"It will be," the older woman assured, walking over and straightening Ines's collar, and smoothing her hands down her sleeves. "I wouldn't lie to you, girl. He's the right one for you. You two are just what the other needs, in more ways than you could know."

Ines didn't have time to answer, for Aunt Rosemary stepped back just as the door flung open and Joseph walked inside. She quickly turned to the basket to hide any redness in her face.

"Ready?" he asked, grabbing the lunch.

"Yes, I am," Ines said.

"Don't forget your hat," Aunt Rosemary said. "A woman's complexion is one of her most valuable commodities."

Ines simply nodded, and donned the straw hat, tying it under her chin. Once she stepped outside, she was glad Aunt Rosemary had suggested it. The sun beat down terribly now, even though she'd only been inside a short time.

"Need help up?" Joseph asked, pointing to the chestnut mare before her. "I know you city girls probably don't ride much."

Ines smiled, though it was forced, and tried to ignore the comment. "Please," she said instead.

Joseph helped her into the saddle, and Ines grabbed the reins tightly. Joseph shook his head. "Hold them a little looser, or else you'll hurt her mouth,"

"Sorry," Ines mumbled.

Joseph swung up effortlessly, and started to ride. Luckily, her horse followed him. A time or two, he looked over at her, correcting how she sat or held the reins. Fury filled Ines, along with embarrassment. She knew she wasn't perfect. Knew she didn't know what she was doing, but she was trying. Didn't that count for something?

"Sorry." Joseph shrugged. "I can tell you don't like me correcting you. But it's to keep you safe. If your horse were to spook, you don't want to fall off or get dragged, caught in the reins."

"I understand," Ines said, her voice low. She did. He was being reasonable. But she was tired of it. Critical parents, critical Aunt Rosemary, critical Joseph. Maybe this hadn't been a good idea. Not the horse ride, not the picnic, not coming to Oregon at all.

"Things will get easier for you," Joseph said, as they stopped and he swung down from his horse.

Ines stared off into the distance. Would they? "I hope so," she finally said. She met his eyes boldly, and said, "I know I wasn't who you chose, but I assure you, I am doing the best that I can to be who you need."

Chapter 9

Joseph felt a swell of hurt through him. It was obvious Ines misunderstood his earlier comments as a complaint, even an insinuation that she wasn't good enough or who he wanted. He couldn't say contrary to that, exactly, because he hadn't had any say in who he was marrying. That was his own fault. Regardless, he knew the thing to do was apologize.

"I'm sorry," he said quietly. "I know this isn't fair to you. You likely didn't get much say in coming here."

"I'm sure it's not entirely fair for you either," Ines said, accepting his help off of the horse. "After all, you were rushed into this and didn't get to find a wife of your choosing."

"Well, that's where you're wrong," Joseph said. "I had a lot of chances to get a woman, just none caught my eye. And then I mixed up the age I had to get married. Maybe I'd have tried harder if I realized time was getting away from me."

She smiled, though it didn't quite meet her eyes. "Well, time got away from me as well, and here I am. Though my story is a little different. No matter how many men I liked, not a single one liked me."

Ines walked toward a spot, and shook out a blanket from the picnic basket. "Is this fine?"

"Yes," Joseph said, hurrying over, "but what do you mean? No one liked you. I find that hard to believe."

She simply shrugged. "It's the truth. It was my younger sister, Lily, that everyone liked."

"Lily," Joseph said, trying to recall where he'd heard that name. "Didn't you say her name earlier?"

"I did," Ines said, sitting down on the blanket and straightening her skirts. "She eloped on the day she and I were to travel out to meet the man Aunt Rosemary had arranged for her to marry."

"Ohhh hooo," Joseph laughed. "I bet Aunt Rosemary didn't like that."

"My parents especially didn't like that," Ines corrected him. "So, when the offer came for me to come here, my mother was quite excited. She still got to talk about a daughter getting married to a man no one knew about, so she could make up all sorts of fabulous things, and that would hopefully overshadow what my sister did."

"Did any of you see it coming?" Joseph asked, curious. "Her running away?"

Ines paused, then finished setting out the food. As they helped themselves, she said, "I don't think so. She was the pretty one, the popular one. She was also the troublemaker, and got away with a lot, though she didn't ever do anything—until now—that would have been too scandalous."

"And you?" Joseph asked, hoping to learn a little more than he had the night before about his future wife. Now that they were alone, she seemed a little more talkative.

"I'm...plain. Predictable. Boring." Ines looked down at her lap. "That's about it."

"I don't think so," Joseph told her. He inched closer. "If you ask me, you're pretty brave, coming out here all this way with my aunt." When she raised her eyebrows at that, he continued. "Plus, you are a good cook, just from the little I've tasted. You are well spoken, so I bet you like books." At her nod, he continued, "Nothing boring about any of that. Those are all good things. And as for plain..."

Joseph hesitated, then brushed his hand against hers. "I don't think you are plain. I think you're beautiful. Inside and out."

Her eyes flicked to his, and when her cheeks pinked, Joseph reached for her hand and held it. "I understand about feeling like you aren't anything special, when you're the reliable one," he said.

"You do?" Ines asked.

"Sure. I run this ranch. It doesn't leave much time for anything else. Never has. My father warned me about that. That's also likely why he told me to marry before he passed on, because he knew once the place was mine, there would be even less time than I had then."

"It does seem a great deal of work," Ines said. "Your ranch is enormous."

"I hope it stays that way," Joseph sighed. "If my cousin gets his way..."

"He won't," Ines said. "That's why I'm here."

He studied her a moment. "I appreciate that, Ines. But I want you to know that if you are here under duress, if your parents or my aunt are forcing you, then it's okay to say no. I know...I know we got pushed together, and I'm more grateful than you'll ever know that you are here to help me, but I won't force you to say I do."

"I appreciate that," Ines said, taking a deep breath, "but I'm not going to say no."

That didn't exactly make Joseph feel better. She hadn't fully answered straight out if she was being forced here. But he shouldn't have expected her to. She was trapped just like he was. In a difficult situation. She was his last resort. Who knew? Maybe he was hers, too.

Joseph realized Ines had been saying something, and looked over at her. "I'm sorry. Can you repeat that?"

"I was asking if, once you marry, that will solve any future problem of the ranch being yours."

He tensed slightly. Was she already looking for a way out? He had to be prepared for that. A woman such as her, it had to be a lie that she couldn't find a man interested in her. Sure, she was a little older than some, but she wasn't nearly ready to be put out to pasture.

Joseph took a bite before answering. "I have to be married for five years or have two children before there's no risk of losing the ranch."

"What if you have both?" Ines asked, then her cheeks blazed red. "I mean, that is, if you wanted a family."

"I...I will be honest. I hadn't thought too much about that, other than assuming one day I'd have some children to pass this place down to." He glanced at her, then away quickly. "But, whenever you are ready. When we are ready. I know this is sudden, I do. So, I'm fine with a marriage of convenience, if that's what you want."

Ines bit her lip and whispered something so softly, Joseph couldn't hear it. "Can you say that again?" he asked, taking his finger and tipping up her chin.

The softness of her skin against his fingertips felt like what silk must be like. Joseph suddenly wanted to run his hand over her cheek, pull her closer, see how soft her lips were. He pulled his hand away. What was he doing, thinking like that? She was a stranger. A city girl. She likely wouldn't want his rough hands on her.

Ines watched his hand move away. Her eyes were sad as she answered, "I'll do whatever you want. I'm happy with a marriage of convenience, though I hope we'll be friends. Maybe even more one day. I...I always have wanted love."

Love. Ines wanted love. And, why shouldn't she? She deserved it. He did too. Just the situation wasn't one where it was an option. Or...was it? Could they have that one day?

Her sweet face held a worry on it that Joseph wanted to ease. A tinge of fear, perhaps that feeling of being so unwanted she was wary of his response. He knew what that was like. Felt it keenly, after he'd been rejected. Maybe that's part of what kept drawing him to her. He recognized those vulnerable parts in her. They were the same he had. And they spoke of a connection that might grow to more.

"Ines," Joseph said quietly, searching her face as he slowly moved his hand to squeeze hers gently before letting go. "I want that too."

Her smile was genuine, and something seemed to relax inside of Ines. They didn't say anything else at first as they continued to eat, though they snuck several looks at the other. Eventually, they started to talk again, and Joseph found himself more and more attracted to Ines with every passing moment. He especially liked the way she would laugh at his jokes.

Maybe his aunt hadn't just gotten the first woman she saw for him. After all, she had a reputation for making matches. Maybe she'd chosen Ines especially for him. He hoped so.

But at the same time, it scared him. What if Ines didn't adjust? Bess's face appeared in his mind's eye. The twisted expression of disgust on her face, the way she'd shuddered looking about the town. Looking at him.

What if Ines did the same? Worse, what if she did it after he'd fallen in love with her? He wasn't lying. He did want love. The idea scared him because if she did leave him after five years of marriage, once the ranch was safe and she could be free, he didn't know how he'd manage. Without a doubt, he knew life wouldn't be the same without her. He'd hardly known Ines, but already knew he was in danger of losing his heart. He couldn't let that happen.

He had to steel it. This wasn't about love. It was about saving the ranch and making a life with a stranger.

Chapter 10

Ines punched the bread dough and recovered it, then went to check on the cinnamon rolls she had rising on the counter. She'd discovered that Joseph had a sweet tooth, and that delighted her, for it meant she could make all of her favorites as well, and have an excuse to eat them.

Joseph also had a love of reading, something that made Ines hopeful that they'd find other shared interests. He showed her where his study was, and pointed out an entire wall filled with books, telling her to read whatever she liked. She'd selected two titles that sounded interesting. One was a history book about France, the other a book on gardening. She figured she'd best learn more about that.

Yesterday evening, Aunt Rosemary had settled herself at the kitchen table with one of her books and a pencil, frantically scribbling away. Ines wondered what she was writing down. She'd quickly lost her curiosity, though, as Joseph had invited Ines onto the porch with him to watch the sunset.

They hadn't spoken much, just watched the glorious reds and oranges turn to dusky purples and blues, but there had been something else in the air that Ines couldn't quite explain. It felt similar to when he'd touched her face and her hand that day at their picnic. It made her want more of that feeling.

"Ines, we will go to the dressmaker after lunch," Aunt Rosemary called through the window, where she was outside, collecting flowers for a small bouquet for her bedroom.

"That sounds wonderful," Ines said. "There are a few sundries I'd like to get at the general store too."

When there was no reply, her thoughts flitted back to Joseph. What would it be like once they were married? He seemed a kind and thoughtful man and, even though neither of them had chosen the other, that didn't seem to matter. Somehow, they'd fallen into easy conversation each time they spoke, and Ines had the strangest feeling that she'd known him forever.

She wondered if he felt the same. If that might make it easier for them to be friends. And more. Yet, though she was relaxing a little more around him, he still seemed tense. Careful.

The kitchen door opened, and Aunt Rosemary quickly closed it behind her. "That dog of his," she muttered. "The beastly creature just won't leave me alone."

Ines stifled a laugh. It was true. The dog had taken quite a liking to the older woman, following her about whenever she was outdoors. "I think she just senses you are a good person," Ines said.

"I am, aren't I?" Aunt Rosemary agreed with a smile. "I'm going to look for something in my trunk, dear. I'll be back in a while."

Ines nodded, and slid the cinnamon rolls into the oven. She glanced around the kitchen. Since they were going into town, she wanted to make a list of the things they were almost out of. She liked how quickly Joseph had allowed her to take over the running of the home, and encouraged her to get anything she might want. He seemed to trust her, which she appreciated. There might not be love, but perhaps there was respect forming.

"Let's see, where did Joseph say he kept the paper and pencils?" Ines asked herself, as she opened the kitchen drawers one by one to peer inside.

In the third drawer, she spotted some paper. As she dug around for something to write with, her fingers brushed against a small photograph of a lovely woman with light-colored curls. Was this a relative, perhaps? Ines flipped it over, and saw the name Bess written on the back.

Bess. Wasn't that the woman who Joseph had been going to marry? She swallowed. Why did he have her photograph still? Maybe...maybe he'd forgotten he had it? Or maybe he still held some sort of affection for her?

She studied it for a long moment. The woman had a lovely face, a clear complexion, and long fingers. Her figure was slim, her nose tiny, and... she was perfect. Every inch of her. The complete opposite of who Ines was. She glanced down at her work-worn fingers, her dress that was only suitable, not stunning, and slowly put the photograph back into the drawer, grabbing the pencil she now spotted.

Taking a deep breath, she closed her eyes for a moment. Just because he had the picture still didn't mean anything. Or so she wanted to believe. But now that she'd seen what Bess looked like, Ines felt nothing but all of her faults, glaring loudly at her. She wasn't nearly so lovely. There was no way that Joseph would ever love her, not when he could have had a woman such as Bess.

The kitchen was hot from the oven, and Ines opened the back door, to cool it and herself down a little. She was about to walk away when she heard men talking. Curious, she glanced through the door to see Joseph talking to a man in a suit. She started to turn away, not wanting to seem that she was eavesdropping, until she heard her name.

"Ines Martin? Don't know her. Think you'll hold on to her longer than the last one?" the man in the suit laughed.

"That's none of your concern," Joseph said, almost in a growl.

"But it is. I'm your lawyer. It's my job to make sure you have a wife by your birthday and if you don't, to sign the place over to your cousin."

His lawyer. So that's who it was. Ines hesitated. She wasn't sure if going over would help or make things worse.

The lawyer continued, "Are you sure this Ines exists? I've not seen anyone new in town."

Ines could see Joseph's jaw clench, and she decided it didn't matter what anyone thought. She refused to let that man bother Joseph and accuse him of lying. Leaving the kitchen, she went over to them, smiling at the men as she approached, and then wrapped her arm around Joseph's. "I'm sorry to interrupt. Joseph, I have cinnamon rolls in the oven. Would you like a few before I go into town and do my shopping?"

"I'd love that," Joseph said, smiling back at her. He glanced at the lawyer. "Mr. Altrose, this is Ines, my soon-to-be wife. My aunt is chaperoning us until we are wed."

"Hello," Ines said. "It's good to meet you."

"And you," the lawyer said. Then he asked, "How are you finding the place?"

"It's wonderful," Ines said honestly. "I love it here."

That didn't seem to be what he expected, as surprise formed on his face. "That so? Well, good."

"If you'll excuse me, I'm going to check the oven," Ines said, and turned toward the house.

"What will you do if the other woman comes back?" Mr. Altrose asked, nearly making Ines stumble. He hadn't even seemed to care she was still there, and within earshot. Ines looked over her shoulder, but his question was directed at Joseph, not her.

"Why do you think that is a possibility?" Joseph asked.

"Stranger things have happened," the lawyer said with a shrug, and a smile Ines didn't care for.

"Good afternoon, Mr. Altrose," Joseph said, and caught up with her.

Inside, Ines pulled the sweet rolls from the oven, and tried to ignore the churning in her stomach. She knew they shouldn't, but the lawyer's words had upset her. Joseph seemed to pick up on that.

"What's wrong?" he asked her as she drizzled icing over the still-hot rolls.

"Nothing. Just...something about that man. I didn't care for him," she admitted, not wanting to tell him she'd heard the last part of their conversation, which obviously wasn't meant for her.

"I feel the same," Joseph said. He scowled. "He doesn't act like my lawyer. He acts like he's on my cousin's side."

"Is he?" Ines asked, her eyes searching his face. What a terrible thing it would be if the man was.

"I hope not," Joseph told her. He sighed deeply. "I'm sure it's nothing. That's probably just the way lawyers are. Like to act like they know everything."

Ines nodded, as she slid two cinnamon rolls onto a plate. "I'm sure you are right," she said, as she went to pour Joseph a mug of milk.

But fear had taken hold of her at the lawyer's final words. What *would* Joseph do if the other woman came back? It seemed an unlikely situation. After all, what woman rejects someone and then returns to them? But then again, why would he have said that, unless it was a possibility? Did the lawyer know something they didn't? It was possible, too, that Joseph wanted her to return. After all, he still had her photograph. That had to mean something.

Ines set about the dishes to hide her trembling hands. Joseph didn't need her. He only needed a wife. That meant she was replaceable. Ines had just started to feel comfortable here. At home. Making plans for the future.

A future that now might not even exist for her. She was foolish to even think that might happen. A heavy weight of despair filled her, as the memory of Bess's lovely face filled her mind. Why in the world would Joseph choose someone like her, when he could have Bess?

Chapter 11

Joseph had liked when Ines came up to him outside and wrapped her arm through his. It had felt right. Natural. Despite his determination to not fall in love with Ines, she was making it difficult.

When she moved away to go back to the house, he felt her absence keenly. And then when Mr. Altrose had made the comment about Bess returning, he hadn't missed the stricken expression on Ines's face. Nor the sharp pain that shot through his chest at the idea.

He didn't want Bess to return. Not at all. She'd made it abundantly clear she wasn't interested in him or the town. But...something about the way the lawyer had said it, and about how he'd know, just didn't set right with him. Ines had seemed to feel the same.

So, what did that mean? Could it be that the lawyer was, in some way, responsible for Bess leaving? He didn't see how that could be, for he didn't think they knew each other, but now that the seed of doubt had been planted, it started to sprout in his gut and grow quickly, with prickles all over it.

Now, he wished Ines hadn't mentioned she was going to town. And he wished he'd never said her name. He knew that was likely a foolish thing to worry over, but as he watched Ines, the plant of fear within him blossomed a disturbing thought. What if Bess had been enticed away? Or threatened? And what if Ines was next? Was she in danger?

The thought made him stand, scraping his chair back. He was going to warn Cal. Ask him and the others to keep an eye on the place.

Ines glanced over at him as she dried her hands on her apron. "I'm going to the garden for a few moments before Aunt Rosemary and I go to town," she said, smiling at him, though the smile failed to meet her eyes, just as she failed to meet his.

"These are really good," Joseph said, indicating the remaining cinnamon rolls.

Their eyes locked, and she whispered, "Thank you."

Time seemed to freeze, and if it hadn't been for the sound of one of his men outside hollering about something, Joseph felt like it was one of those moments where he should walk over, pull her into his arms, and kiss her.

"I'll go get a wagon ready," Joseph said abruptly. "I can't take you to town, as I've got to take possession of a head of cattle coming any moment, but I'll have one of the hands drive you."

"That's appreciated," Ines said. "I'm not sure Aunt Rosemary would care for such a walk, and I don't know how to drive a wagon yet."

"It's not hard at all, and I'll teach you," Joseph promised.

She nodded, and went outside.

Joseph watched her through the window for a moment. She wandered the rows of plants, inspecting one here or there. Her shoulders were slumped. What was she feeling? He knew it couldn't be easy for her right now. At all, really.

His eyes fell on a book sitting on the counter. He couldn't help but smile. Had she propped it there to read while making the cinnamon rolls?

He let himself out the kitchen door, and Storm ran up to him. "Where's Cal?" he asked the dog. With a bark, the dog answered, and ran toward the barn. Joseph found his foreman there, bent over a horse inspecting a small wound.

"Look okay?" Joseph asked.

"She'll be fine," Cal said. "Got nicked on a nail that came out of the wall."

Joseph looked at the horse himself, and then dabbed some ointment on the small cut. "I need you to do something," he said.

"Sure thing, boss." Cal wiped his forehead. "What do you need?"

"I have a bad feeling," Joseph said. "Like something might happen to Ines. I can't explain it, and maybe it's nothing. Maybe it's just nerves, worries that something will prevent the marriage. The lawyer was here, and you know how he sets me on edge. I don't know. But..."

"Don't worry. I'll let the men know to keep an eye out in case they see any strangers. Especially if that lawyer comes back. I get a bad feeling about him," Cal said. "But don't you worry. We'll keep her safe. Your aunt too."

"Thank you," Joseph said. He glanced out the barn window toward the garden. He didn't see Ines, and for some reason he couldn't understand, that worried him. Maybe it was because he'd just been talking to Cal, but he wanted to see her. Even just a glimpse, and make sure she was okay.

"Cal, my aunt and Ines need to go into town. Can you hitch the wagon and have someone drive them there and back?"

"Will do that myself," Cal said.

Joseph thanked him, and went to look for Ines. He unlatched the garden gate and went in. Some of the plants were tall, so she must be behind one of those. Joseph walked among the vines of beans, down the path of tall corn, and past the cabbages. He didn't see Ines anywhere. He was just about to turn and see if she'd gone back to the house, when he heard the softest of sounds.

He followed the noise, which had turned into quiet sobs, and found Ines sitting on the ground, her arms around her knees and partially hidden by the wheelbarrow. She hadn't noticed him.

Slowly, so as not to frighten her, Joseph approached, and then he sat next to her. It was the most natural thing in the world to put his arm around her shoulders and pull her close.

Maybe it was time to stop fighting himself. Joseph closed his eyes. He couldn't let what had happened make him fearful over the future. Life was already uncertain enough, without inviting more worry.

Ines's tears dampened his shirt, but he didn't care. He reached one hand up to stroke her head, and her soft hair. "Ines, tell me what's wrong," Joseph pleaded. "Has something happened? Have...have I done something?"

She shook her head. "It's nothing. And no, you haven't. Not yet, anyway."

"Tell me," he begged, pulling back slightly to see her tearstained face.

"You don't understand," she said softly.

"And I never will, if you don't tell me," he said. "But if something is wrong, let me help. Let me take care of you.

You are going to be my wife. That means something to me. It means that I have a responsibility to protect you, to care for you."

"Is that all I'll be?" Ines asked. "A responsibility?" Her face held disappointment.

"No, I-I want to take care of you. Be there for you. Help you." Joseph didn't know why he was stammering. He sensed there was a lot more to her question than he was picking up on.

Ines stared off across the garden. Joseph tried to follow her gaze but didn't see anything but the cucumber plants. Finally, she sighed. He turned back to her, giving her his full attention.

"What if..." Ines stopped. "I saw the picture. On accident. I was looking for a pencil. But it was in the drawer next to it."

"Picture?" Joseph asked. He shook his head and gave a small frown. "What picture?"

"Of Bess," Ines said. "She's very pretty. Seeing it was a surprise. And it just...I don't know. And then the lawyer...I didn't mean to overhear him, but I did. Now, all I can think about is if...if she does come back, will you leave me for her? I know that this is just a marriage of convenience, for both of us. But I...I am falling in love with you, and I want you to know that."

Before he could answer, she added, "But if she does come back, if you do want to be with her, I won't cause a problem. I'll leave. I want you to be happy. To have what you want. Even if it's not me."

Ines stood then, and rushed out of the garden and into the house. Joseph stood, half in shock. How was it she thought he wanted someone else?

And worse, what was he going to do to convince her otherwise?

Chapter 12

Ines couldn't believe she'd just said what she had when they were in the garden. She sounded so desperate! What must he think of her? It was no wonder she didn't have any experience in relationships. She likely scared others away. If Joseph weren't in the situation he had found himself in, chances were she would have scared him off as well.

Angrily, she splashed cold water on her face, trying to diminish the redness on her cheeks and in her eyes. From embarrassment or anger or hurt, she wasn't sure, but unfortunately, her skin reacted the same way each time, a blotchy pink and red that stained her entire face.

Ines groaned as she dabbed at her face with a soft towel and then fanned it, trying to fade the marks. Who told someone they hardly knew that they were falling in love with them? She'd been so bold! Too bold. What was wrong with her? Men didn't like that. They liked women like her sister. Pretty and giggling, with fluttering eyelashes and always letting men come to the rescue. That wasn't her. But then, who was she? How was she supposed to act here? She'd been trying so hard to learn all she could to be a help here on the ranch. Was that the wrong thing to do?

Being here on a ranch, taking care of oneself was an important skill. But did that mean that Joseph would just think of her as another set of hands around the place instead of a woman? She was sure if Bess had still been there, she wouldn't have been seen that way.

A woman with hands like Bess had in the photograph wouldn't do anything domestic. Not cook, not clean. Ines looked down at her fingers. Would Joseph have gotten Bess a housekeeper if she couldn't cook? A personal maid? He hadn't offered either of those to her.

Ines didn't want those things; she also didn't need them. But she did want to feel special. Important. Be asked if she wanted something like that. Have someone think about what she might like. And she wasn't sure if Joseph felt concerned in that way about her. She wouldn't blame him if he didn't. After all, she wasn't his first pick for a wife.

What would it feel like to come in first? To not be second all the time, be unwanted? She let herself think about that for a moment, as she changed dresses and washed her face and hands.

To be chosen...desired. To have others laugh when she made a joke, even if it wasn't funny. To rush to open a door for her, help her across the street. Tell her how lovely she was. When there was a social event, vie for her attention and the chair nearest hers. And dances...if there was one, to have her card full, to not be passed over, but to have one man after another eager and anxious for his turn with her.

Then there were the surprises her sister always got. A note from an admirer. Flowers. Sweets. Small things that were heartfelt.

That would be lovely. Ines let herself smile at the thought. But then she frowned. Because she'd often been on the sidelines, she'd watched the others her age and younger. Women who didn't always like their dance partners, but tolerated them. Women who were paraded about, like they were animals at the market. Men, who treated them as though they were a possession or an accessory.

It seemed that often, to have the one thing, you had to have the other. Ines didn't want that. And...and Joseph hadn't treated her like that. In fact, he'd been genuine in his compliments, especially about her cooking. He hadn't treated her as though she weren't smart enough to follow along with what he'd said.

For example, the first night there, when he'd talked about the issue with the lawyer and the ranch, he'd answered her questions, and those from his aunt, as though they were equals. He didn't try and simplify or leave anything out, thinking they weren't capable of understanding.

As for door holding, he had done that. He'd also pulled out her chair at dinner, but hadn't expected her to wait on him. He'd treated her as an equal, yet someone who was important to him.

She liked that.

So, why didn't she try and get more of it? Why hadn't she ever tried? She was deserving of such things too. Yet, she always stopped herself somehow. Stood on the sidelines, willingly. Let her sister have the spotlight. Told herself that she was doing the right thing. The kind thing.

But what if it wasn't? What if she'd actually been part, if not all, of the problem? Been the one to reject the attentions of others out of some strange sense of self sacrifice for her sister?

Ines studied her reflection in the small mirror, moving this way and that to see as much of herself as possible. A sudden memory of her sister doing the same the morning she'd left while Ines sat on the bed sprang to her mind.

Lily. Lily had gone after what she wanted. Love. It didn't matter to her what others had said. Didn't matter that it wasn't right, by society's rules. That she could be seen as compromised both by leaving and if things didn't work out. She'd gone after what her heart had told her to do. In fact, her whole life she'd done that. Maybe Lily didn't always choose correctly, but she followed her dreams. It was a good lesson. And one that Ines hoped wasn't too late to learn.

The difference, however, between her and her sister was that Ines knew actions had consequences. Her sister's rash decision to run away had left the family in turmoil. She had been thoughtless. Ines couldn't do that. She couldn't hurt her family. Or Joseph. But she could, hopefully, make a life for herself that would be pleasing, and not cause others to have to pick up the pieces or scramble to make things right for another.

Here, in the West, people created new destinies for themselves all the time. Wasn't that why so many people braved the hardships to get here? The chance for a fresh start? A reinvention of oneself? She could do that too.

Determination, and something akin to excitement, filled Ines. She could do this. She could have her new beginning, the future that she made.

And that future would include Joseph, because Ines wanted him. If Bess came back, she wouldn't let her have him. Not without a fight. She wanted to stay here in Oregon, wanted to be with Joseph, and wanted her happily ever after that Aunt Rosemary seemed so sure she'd have.

Now, she just had to figure out how to make that happen, and not talk herself out of going after what she wanted and take her usual place on the sidelines.

Chapter 13

Joseph stood, staring at the spot where Ines had been but a moment before. Her words had sliced through him. She was falling in love with him, but she'd give him up, if that's what would make him happy.

Almost feeling numb, he staggered into the house. What was he to do? How did he reply to that? He didn't know what he was doing. What to say to make things better, to set her mind at ease. What if he made things worse? Was it better to just be silent?

He wasn't even sure how he felt. There was still that worry that Ines would leave. That she'd be unhappy here. He wished there was someone to tell him what to do.

His parents had always made it look so easy. So did just about every other couple he ever saw. No one told him that a relationship with someone might be anything but.

From his spot in the kitchen, Joseph stared at her closed bedroom door. He hoped Ines wasn't crying. He'd be able to hear if she was, wouldn't he? But what was he supposed to do if she was?

His aunt came into the kitchen, and saw where his gaze was. She pressed her lips together. "That girl hasn't had it easy," she finally said. "Always overlooked. The best of the two, not that anyone bothered to notice."

"Why do you think that is?" Joseph asked, still staring at Ines's door.

"Because her sister was outgoing. One of those girls who was pretty and knew it. That could—and did—lead to trouble, and her parents paid extra attention to her, trying to calm her down. I told them that marriage they were sending her to wouldn't work to settle her. But they begged me to find her someone. Anyone. I wish they'd listened."

"And I understand it didn't even happen," Joseph said, walking back to the table to grab a dirty plate and put it in the wash pail.

"No, it didn't," his aunt said thoughtfully. "Eventually, had Lily gone, I think she'd have found contentment. He'd have been good for her. Perhaps she'd have matured enough to see that. But even still, Ines's parents don't realize that you cannot force a connection between two individuals. That one can have both the goal and the outcome if it's done correctly."

"I'm not sure I understand," he said.

His aunt pressed her lips together. "Ines lacks confidence in herself because of her upbringing. She's always been second best. Often not even chosen. Sometimes because she thought that was best and what others expected of her, as she let her sister shine. After a time, that kind of self sacrifice wears a person down."

"I have never really experienced anything like that," Joseph said quietly. "I guess out here, there are fewer opportunities for the social aspects that would create such things. But when I was rejected for marriage, it sure did hurt. Made me wonder what was wrong with me. Still does."

"Imagine that for years," his aunt said. She gave him a considering look. "I didn't choose Ines for you on a whim. I chose her because you are meant for each other. I just hope the two of you discover how."

"But I don't know how," Joseph said, frustration and despair filling him. "I don't know how to be married. What to do. How to convince her that I do like her. Want her here. Could love her. Maybe even do."

"No one does until the time comes," his aunt told him. "But, you will do a fine job, Joseph. I am sure of it."

"So you say," Joseph answered and crossed his arms over his chest. "You seem so confident in it. But, I'm not."

His aunt was quiet. "There's nothing wrong with you," his aunt told him. "Even though you live in this rough and dusty place, you are a fine man, with potential for so much. The woman who rejected you was a fool, and it's her loss."

"She wouldn't have lasted here," Joseph said. "All frills and curls. Ines isn't as fussy, but I still have my doubts. She's a city girl. Not used to this kind of life."

"You'd be surprised what a woman can do for the right man," his aunt said, fixing him with her sharp eyes. Before he could answer, she glanced toward Ines's door. "I feel for Ines," she said. "Always passed over, always accepting that. It isn't that the girl doesn't have a backbone. It's that she is willing to sacrifice herself for what others want."

Her words stilled Joseph. Hadn't Ines said something just a few moments ago to prove that? That she'd leave, if he wanted Bess?

"She's just like you in many ways," his aunt continued. "After all, weren't you willing to sacrifice your own happiness and be rejected for the sake of keeping the ranch in your family? Not even once, but twice if the next woman turned out uninterested in you? That's why I brought you Ines. I searched hard for her. Why, I gave myself eyestrain and numerous papercuts. Do you know how long it took me to put my books away, after all the young women I researched? But she will make you happy. She is a woman who will do anything for the man she loves."

"I just hope I can make her happy, prove to her that she belongs here," Joseph said. "Even if love doesn't happen right away, I don't want her to feel unwanted."

There was the soft sound of Ines's door opening, and she appeared in the kitchen doorway. "I'm ready, Aunt Rosemary," she said, not looking at him.

"Good. Let us venture forth and see what this barren place has in the way of material and a dressmaker," his aunt said. "Joseph, is someone driving us? Or must we take our lives into our own hands? It has been years since I drove my pony cart as a girl."

"Yes, you'll be driven. Let me go get Cal and the wagon," Joseph said. He hurried outside.

Ines and his aunt were right behind him, and he helped them into the wagon, not wanting to release Ines's hand. He squeezed it gently, and was pleased to see her blush slightly.

"Get whatever you want," he said, meeting Ines's eyes. "Anything. I mean that. For yourself, for the house. Whatever you see. Put it on my account."

"Oh, she will," his aunt said. "I'll see to that. You are severely lacking in comforts here. Your soap has no scent!"

He would have replied, maybe smiled, kissed Ines's hand he still held, Joseph wasn't sure what, but Cal shook the reins, and the wagon sped off, separating them, and jolting in a way he was sure his aunt would complain about later.

Joseph watched until the wagon and its passengers were a small speck. He wasn't sure if it was just wishful thinking or his imagination, but he could have sworn the smaller of the figures, Ines, turned around and waved. His heart hopeful, he raised his hand in return.

When she came back, he was going to do the best he could to let Ines know he was going to make her happy. Make her a good husband.

As the wagon vanished from view, a worrying feeling filled his stomach. Joseph tried to ignore it, but it grew, despite his best efforts to reassure himself all was well.

Just a bit of jitters. His aunt was going into the town he was sure she wouldn't approve of, he finally told himself, hoping it was the truth. It had nothing to do with the fact he didn't like Ines being without him.

Chapter 14

"Not the yellow," Aunt Rosemary said. "Nor the sage. You'll look dreadful in those."

Ines, thankfully, wasn't interested in either of those colors. She did have her eye on the display of blue fabrics, in several shades. "What of these?" she asked, running a finger along one that reminded her of the wildflowers she'd seen when she first arrived.

Aunt Rosemary studied it for a moment, holding a corner of the fabric to Ines's cheek. "I think this will do nicely. Though, I don't understand why you won't visit the dressmaker, and insist on making the dress yourself."

"I've already told you," Ines said softly, turning toward the lace pieces, where she studied them to find something in a design she liked for her cuffs and collar, "it will give me something to do over the next few days. Besides, I enjoy sewing."

When there was no reply, she looked up, but Joseph's aunt was across the shop near the beauty products and soaps, squinting at something on a shelf that Ines couldn't see.

The first thing she'd done when they arrived in town today was post an urgent message to her lawyer, asking him to look into the situation with Joseph's ranch, his lawyer, and his cousin. Truthfully, Ines was glad that she had. The entire situation didn't sit right with her. Something about the lawyer felt...off. Though she'd never met another to compare him to, her instincts told her he was a man to be wary of.

Aunt Rosemary had agreed, and warned her if she ran into the man again, to be just as she was before. Pleasant, cautious, and sweet. Not to raise any alarm, or potentially make the situation worse.

Ines glanced again at the older woman, who had now moved to a row of blank books, looking at them with a pleased expression. Would those end up on the shelves in her room back home, filled with the names and details of those who lined the pages?

With no objection given to her fabric choice, Ines decided upon the rest of what she wanted for her dress, including some new sewing needles and pins. She went to the sales counter and set them down. "There are a few other things I'd like," she told the woman behind the counter. Earlier, the woman had introduced herself as the shop's owner, and had been very attentive. "Do you mind if I set these here while I browse?"

"Of course," the woman said. "And shall I cut you a dress length?"

Aunt Rosemary was at her elbow before Ines could answer. "That's a new bolt, isn't it? Have you sold any to anyone else?"

"No," the shop owner said. "You'll be the first."

"Then she'll take it all," Aunt Rosemary said. "In a small town such as this, a woman needs to have something all her own no other woman has, even if it's simply the fabric."

Ines opened her mouth to argue, but the shop owner nodded briskly. "I quite agree. You'll find," she added to Ines, "most of the women do just that. The extra gets used for aprons or curtains, or even just to save by in case something happens to a sleeve or hem."

"Tell me about those lotions," Aunt Rosemary said, gesturing to a shelf. "My skin is too dry here."

As the two women went to look at the lotions and soaps, Ines took the opportunity to stroll through the store, breathing in deeply.

For a small town, this store had just about everything a person could want. There were fabrics and all the needed notions, foodstuffs, dishes and bakeware, and a good selection of things for both home and comfort. She would enjoy shopping here.

A soft bell over the door tinkled, but Ines didn't glance its way. After all, she wouldn't know anyone else in this town. She'd only just arrived. Once she and Joseph married, she was sure that would change, and he'd introduce her around. For now, they'd agreed that they wanted to be quiet about the fact she was here and going to marry him. It was no one's business but their own. And the lawyer's, of course.

"Ines, dear," Aunt Rosemary called. "Which do you prefer for hand soap at the house? Lilac scented or lavender? There is rose and honeysuckle as well. One of each to see?"

The sound of heavy footsteps drawing close to her prevented Ines from answering. A man stood in front of her, near her age, but with a smirk that made him look more like a spoiled child. She'd known men like him back home, conceited, thinking only of themselves, and had never liked them. "Ines, are you?" he asked. "Here to marry Joseph McAllen?"

Ines stilled. Warning bells were ringing in her mind, but she tried to still them. Be polite. How had he known? "Yes," she said. "And you are?"

"Hester Smith," he told her, extending a hand, which Ines accepted out of habit. "Joseph's cousin," he added.

His cousin! Ines now wished she hadn't shaken his hand. It was soft. Felt overly large, slightly damp, and it wouldn't release hers. Finally, she tugged it free. It took all she had in her not to wipe it down her skirt. She didn't care which soap Aunt Rosemary bought. Whatever it was, it would take at least a half bar to get her hand clean and remove the feeling of his disgusting touch, she was sure.

"It's good to meet you," she answered, not meaning a word of it, but hoping she looked and sounded sincere.

"How are you finding the town?" he asked her

"It's lovely. I look forward to exploring more of it," Ines answered, wishing he would leave and not keep talking to her.

"Westover is a nice place too," he said, and motioned to the window. "Three stage stops that way. Larger town. Better suited for someone like you."

"Oh no," Ines said, giving a nervous laugh. "I rather like small towns. I wouldn't want to go there. But, I will ask Joseph about it. Perhaps sometime we can take a trip there to see it."

"You could go now," Hester told her. "A thousand dollars. The stage leaves in an hour. No one has to know. You'll just get on it, start over, be a woman of means."

Ines wasn't sure how to react. Instinct would have had her gasp or get angry. But something deep inside tamped down those emotions instead, warning her to put on an impassive expression.

"Why would I want to do that?" she asked.

Had Hester been involved with Bess leaving? Did Joseph know? And, perhaps even more importantly, did the lawyer know? Ines looked around for Cal, Joseph's foreman. He had said he'd be getting a haircut at the barber. He must not have finished yet.

Ines fought back trembles as Hester eyed her from the top of her head to the soles of her boots. His gaze was accompanied by a look in his eyes that made her feel nauseous. "A pretty woman like you deserves better. So, here's another option, since you don't want to leave."

"What's that?" Ines nearly whispered.

From the corner of her eye, she saw Aunt Rosemary starting to come closer. She was both relieved and suddenly worried. Aunt Rosemary sometimes said things that could get under another's skin. What if she did that today? The situation felt precarious.

Hester licked his lips slowly. "You marry me. We'll go, right now, to the preacher. I promise, you'll live a life of luxury. You don't need to keep yourself on that smelly ranch. I own a bank. You will never want for anything."

"Ines," Aunt Rosemary said, appearing at her elbow, "I think we'd best be heading back. Our driver is outside waiting for us."

"No," Hester said. He reached out and grabbed Ines's arm. His fingers dug into her flesh with a strength she wouldn't have expected.

"Let me go," Ines said. Her eyes flashed. "Now."

"Not until you've chosen one of the offers I made," Hester said, his voice cold. "Leave on the stage, or marry me."

Aunt Rosemary gasped. "She'll do no such thing. She's already promised to someone. I know this is a backwards town, but do you men have no manners?"

"This is Hester," Ines said, trying silently to send the older woman a message to be careful. "Joseph's cousin."

Sharp eyes looked him up and down, and then she nodded slowly. "I see."

"He...he would like me to reconsider my stay here, as you heard," Ines said.

"That's right," Hester told her.

"Do you mind letting me go?" Ines asked. "It's hard to think when my arm hurts."

"Of course," he told her with a smirk. "Which of those choices sounds most appealing?"

Just as he asked, the store's door opened, and Cal came in whistling. He froze when he saw Hester.

Aunt Rosemary took the opportunity to pull Ines toward her. "We are leaving," she said firmly.

"No, you aren't," Hester said. He raised the walking stick he carried with him, and aimed it at the older woman.

Ines wasn't sure if he meant to threaten her, or if he simply was brandishing it as a warning that he could—and would—hurt them if he wanted to.

But the sneer on his face showed he didn't care, and he would strike whoever was in his path if he didn't get what he wanted. Hester suddenly swung his walking stick. There was no time to think, but Ines refused to see Aunt Rosemary hurt. She threw herself before Joseph's aunt, pushing her backward enough that the walking stick missed the older woman.

As the blow struck Ines's head, her eyesight began to dim. Everything was spinning, and the shouts and scuffling sound she heard seemed so far away. Ines raised her hand to rub at the ache in her temple, hopefully ease it, but her fingers felt sticky. Warm.

Something was running down her face, but she couldn't wipe it away. Her arms felt too heavy, and her legs too weak. They wouldn't hold her weight any longer, and Ines felt the hard floor below her as she collapsed heavily. She closed her eyes to stop the dizzying and blurry sensation, and that was the last thing she knew.

Chapter 15

Joseph grunted as his pencil rolled off of his desk. Crawling on his hands and knees, he reached for it, banging his head against the top of the desk accidentally. He rubbed at the sore spot, and then awkwardly scooted backward, the pencil in hand.

Then, he stopped. The pencil wasn't the only thing that had fallen off the desk at some point. There was an envelope, partially yellowed with age. Curious, he flattened himself to avoid striking his head again, and reached for the paper.

A moment later, Joseph was sitting back at his desk—which had been his father's, and his father's before him—staring at a letter addressed to himself, from his father.

His mouth went bone dry. It had been four years now, since his father had passed. Three since his mother had followed him of a broken heart. How long had this letter been there? And why had he never received it?

Taking a deep breath, Joseph slowly worked the seal loose and unfolded the single sheet of paper inside. His father's familiar handwriting brought moisture to his eyes, and he sniffled. "Father," he said quietly. "I miss you."

Joseph waited until the blurring of his eyes stopped, then began to read.

Son,

I've been keeping a secret from you. The doctor says I likely don't have too long. Of all the regrets I have in my life, the largest two are glaring at me right now, and there's no time to make amends.

The first is that I wasn't able to spend more time with you and your mother because the ranch took up so much of my time. It wasn't until too late that I realized the value in allowing others to help, and started to hire more men.

The second thing is that I don't know if I have made you understand just how important it is to not be alone in this world. Running the ranch is going to be hard work. You need someone by your side who you can trust, who you can love. Someone to be a partner to you. That person to make your house a home and a place to rest when you are weary.

You won't get that, son, by spending every ounce of your energy working on the ranch. You need to be wed. So, forgive me, my boy, but I made a change to the will. To ensure that you don't wait too long, I changed the age for you to marry from thirty-five to thirty-two.

The lawyer will deliver this letter to you upon my death, and this will serve as your notice that you need to take finding a wife, a partner, someone to love, seriously.

Life is short, and sometimes it ends unexpectedly. You need to make the most of it.

I love you, Joseph, and only want what's best for you. I hope that you can forgive me, but also find a wife who will love you the way that you deserve.

Your loving father

Joseph swallowed hard. Emotions flooded him. He hadn't been mistaken. His father had changed the age of the will for him to marry. And likely because he knew Joseph would put things off until the last minute. Not take the idea of marriage seriously.

It had happened anyway, though, as the letter had been lying there, against the wall, for years.

He could have had four years to find a wife. Instead of simply weeks. Joseph didn't know what to think. How to feel about that. But his practical side won out. No matter what he thought, there was nothing he could do to change the past.

His father's words replayed in his mind as he spoke of his regrets. Of how time was too short. It was true. Time seemed to move so slowly as a child, but then sped up the older he grew. But being forced to marry sooner...it made him angry. Not at his father, no, but because his father knew him too well. Knew Joseph would always put the ranch first, even if that prevented him from marrying.

Love. His father had kept using the word love. Ines had said she was falling in love with him. But he hadn't answered. Love. It was something he could feel for her, but would he? Did he?

He stared at the letter, then slowly returned it to the envelope. Joseph was leaving the study when he heard the wagon returning, at a pace faster than it should have.

Something was wrong. He was hurrying to the door when he heard voices shouting his name. Cal, and...Aunt Rosemary?

Her voice was shrill, fearful.

He rushed through the front door, panic filling every fiber of his being, and he stumbled off the porch and to the wagon.

Cal and his aunt were both talking at the same time, but Joseph couldn't understand anything, except for the words "doctor" and "Ines."

He looked at the back of the wagon, where his aunt was sitting. It was only then he realized that, cradled in her lap, was Ines's head, with dried blood matted in her hair and on her forehead. Her complexion was a sickly pale, her eyes closed, and her breaths shallow.

"What happened?" Joseph asked hoarsely.

"That no-good cousin of yours. He was trying to get Miss Ines to marry him or run away. She said no. She and your aunt started to leave, and he aimed for Miss Rosemary here with that walking stick of his," Cal said, jumping down from the wagon and climbing into the back. "Ines stepped in front of him."

"She saved me," his aunt said tearfully, "that foolish girl! But I don't know if she'll be okay. The doctor has been called for. He's away. All we can do is wait. Try to treat her here. He injured her arm as well, but the head is more severe. I will press charges the moment I see the sheriff. I wish I'd been faster with my Derringer."

"I will press charges as well," Joseph said grimly. Then, the rest of his aunt's sentence sank in. "Wait, you have a Derringer?"

"A woman can never be too careful," his aunt sniffed. "And you can bet I will be buying Ines one as well."

"I approve," Cal grunted. "That scoundrel. Like to have taken care of him myself. But Miss Ines was too important to delay."

Cal carefully picked up Ines, and handed her to Joseph. His aunt hurried before him and pulled back the blankets on Ines's bed.

"Were there witnesses?" Joseph asked. "Has he been arrested?"

"Yes," Cal assured him. "Two of our hands were nearby at the diner and taking care of it. I expect they'll update us soon. They stayed in town too, to wait on the doc. There were a few others in the store. All promised to give statements."

"What do we do?" Aunt Rosemary asked, as she gently brushed Ines's hair from her temple. "Water? Clean her wound? This is beyond my limited medical skills."

"Yes," Joseph said. "I'll get some water. I'm not sure what to do either, but I do know how to treat someone kicked by a horse or knocked out in a brawl. I'll pretend this is that for now and we will treat it the same. Has she woken?"

"No," his aunt said.

That was the last word spoken until the doctor arrived almost an hour later. He examined Ines, and then shook his head, speaking quietly.

"I can't tell you how bad it is. There's no way for me to see inside and analyze what damage there might be, and whether it's swollen or bleeding. All we can do is wait. Keep her comfortable, pray, and watch."

"What of tea?" Aunt Rosemary asked. "Cooled tea spooned in? Is there one that would help?"

"Won't hurt," the doctor agreed. "You can do some willow bark. As much as she'll tolerate. I'll come back this evening, but come get me sooner if you need me."

"Thank you, Doctor," Joseph said, and led the man outside.

As the doctor's wagon drove away, Joseph returned to the room and settled in the extra chair Cal had brought in. Aunt Rosemary had positioned herself right next to Ines, and had a tray nearby with tea steeping.

Joseph memorized each line of Ines's profile, each hair on her head, every lash of her eye that rested on her cheeks. His eyes sought her chest, watching the uneven rhythm of her breath. He was angry at Hester. How dare he attempt—and succeed—at striking a woman? What had come over him?

His aunt had told him what else Hester had said, and Joseph felt sick to his stomach. He should have been there with them. Should have protected Ines and his aunt. How had Hester known Ines's name? There was only one person other than Cal who did.

Mr. Altrose.

He closed his eyes as the lawyer's face appeared before him. "I will get to the bottom of this," Joseph said. He startled, not realizing he'd spoken out loud.

His aunt met his eyes, and quietly said, "As will I. No stone will be unturned. And Ines will recover. You'll see. I know you are likely worried about the ranch, and your upcoming marriage. But she's a strong young woman. A credit to her family, and to you. She's too special to be taken away from us. Once she's recovered, we will go after your cousin, and that lawyer."

"Hester was arrested quickly," Joseph said. "Having so many witnesses to the assault is in our favor. But none of that will mean anything if Ines..." He stopped. He couldn't speak past the lump in his throat.

"She will wake soon. As I told you, Ines is a strong young woman."

"I hope you are right about Ines's recovery," Joseph said, his own voice quiet. "But it's not about the ranch. That's not important anymore. Ines is. I want her to recover because I don't want it to be too late."

"Too late for what?" his aunt asked. "Your marriage deadline?"

"No." Joseph drew in a shuddering breath. "Too late for me to tell her that I love her."

Chapter 16

Ines knew she had to be dreaming. She was moving too slowly, things looked distorted, and the voices speaking were garbled.

First, there was that horrible Hester. His mouth kept moving, but she wasn't understanding anything that came out of it. His overly large face said it all, though, as he reached for her.

Then, there was Aunt Rosemary. The older woman looked startled. Whether she raised an arm to defend herself or to strike at Hester, Ines wasn't sure. She just knew he was angry, and she wouldn't let him touch Joseph's aunt.

The scene had replayed in her mind so many times, Ines thought she'd never escape the endless loop of it. It reminded her of a child tying a piece of string in a circle to play the game cat's cradle. It just went on and on...like the figure eights her sister used to do on the frozen lake everyone ice-skated at.

Suddenly, her eyes flew open, able to force their way past the heaviness. She wasn't at the general store. She was in bed.

Ines's vision slowly adjusted, allowing her to see it was dusk, or perhaps dawn, outside. The sky's muted rays could have been either. Aunt Rosemary sat in a chair next to her, asleep, and her head was at such an angle, Ines was sure the older woman's neck would be aching.

In the corner of the room, Joseph sat, slumped, his head in his hands, with his elbows on his knees. Ines felt surprised they were both there, but also relieved. It meant Hester couldn't get her, and take her away.

Ines moved slightly, and Aunt Rosemary startled awake instantly. "My dear!" she cried out.

That was enough to send Joseph to the other side of her bed, capturing her hand in his. Ines found herself trying to speak, but her words wouldn't come out. Her throat felt so dry.

"Some tea," Aunt Rosemary said. "One moment."

As she bustled out of the room, Joseph moved closer. "Ines," he whispered. "I'm so glad you are awake. Don't talk, but I...I was so worried about you. How do you feel?"

Ines opened her mouth, but Joseph stopped her. "Wait. Don't talk yet. I'm sorry. Have the tea first. You've been asleep for three days."

That startled her. Three days? So long?

"You need to drink first, rest, and gather yourself so you can speak. You've nothing to fear, though. You are safe." Joseph reached out and stroked her forehead. Ines was sure nothing had ever felt so nice.

Ines wanted their moment to last forever, but Aunt Rosemary bustled in, and set about with a tray of tea and, from the smell of it, broth.

"Let me," Joseph said, and reached for the tea, holding it carefully to Ines's mouth.

She drank slowly. It was the most wonderful thing she'd ever tasted. She was still thirsty, though. Joseph seemed to realize that, and held the broth, offering it to her. Once she'd taken a few sips, Ines leaned back, feeling exhausted. But how could that be? According to Joseph, she'd been in bed for three days.

"What happened?" she asked softly, the words taking more effort than she thought they should.

"That no-good—" Aunt Rosemary started, her eyes blazing so fiercely Ines was surprised the room didn't combust.

"I'll finish," Joseph said, reaching for one of Ines's hands. "What's the last thing you remember?"

Ines thought for a moment. "We were in the store. I'd found the most lovely fabric." She tried to sit up. "My fabric!"

"The store sent it over," Aunt Rosemary assured her.

Ines nodded, relieved. She had to make her dress. There was a wedding that must happen. And she was the bride. She'd wear something older, if she had to, but she didn't want Joseph or Aunt Rosemary to be ashamed of her in an older dress.

"I'd found fabric," she said again, trying to organize her thoughts, and not confuse them with the dream she'd had over and over.

"Hester was there. He—" She gasped, and looked at Joseph, "I think he's responsible for Bess leaving. He offered me money to leave, and then asked for me to marry him."

"Never mind about him," Joseph assured her. "He's been locked up and is being investigated right now."

That made her feel better. Ines nodded, though the slight motion made her head hurt. "And then we...we turned to leave. He was angry. His face was so angry," she whispered. "He swung at Aunt Rosemary." Tears filled her eyes, and her voice wobbled, as she sought the other woman. "Are you hurt? Did he hurt you?"

"No, my dear," Aunt Rosemary said, moving closer, and resting a hand on her arm. "You jumped right in front of me. Took the blow that was meant for me."

Her voice changed then, to a whisper that was nearly ferocious. "I didn't come all this way to have one of my fine matches thwarted by some young upstart who wears the most unflattering shade of brown. And do you know how hard that is? Brown is a neutral color!"

Ines smiled, relieved Joseph's aunt was just fine, and leaned back against her pillow.

"I think we need to let the doctor know she's awake," Aunt Rosemary said, rising from her chair. "I'll go tell Cal."

Joseph nodded. When they were alone, Ines whispered, "Will you...will you stroke my head again?"

He smiled at her, and brought his hand back to her face. Ines closed her eyes and relaxed against him.

Joseph leaned closer, and spoke softly. "I'll do whatever you want. Just rest, and feel better."

Ines wanted to answer, but she was feeling so drowsy. Her eyes were getting harder and harder to keep open. She didn't want to sleep, though. She wanted Joseph to keep talking. To keep comforting her. But she was so tired, her thoughts slowed, a yawn escaped, and before Ines could think or say anything at all, she'd slipped back into sleep, only this time there was the comforting presence of Joseph, right next to her.

Chapter 17

"I can walk, honestly," Ines protested, as Joseph carried her from her room to a rocking chair on the porch.

Tired of being in her room, she'd begged for some fresh air. He didn't want her to walk, though. Ines was still pale, and though she claimed her head didn't ache, and the doctor assured them she was past any danger, Joseph was abundantly careful.

Ines had even tried to cut the fabric for her dress, determined to sew it for their wedding. Aunt Rosemary had interceded, and traveled to town with Cal, first to take it and one of Ines's dresses to the dressmaker for sizing, and now, to pick it up. It was hard to believe in just three days, they would be married. So much had happened since she arrived.

"Can I get you anything?" Joseph asked.

"No, I'm fine. I just like you nearby," Ines said, her cheeks pinking slightly.

"I can do that," Joseph said, sitting next to her.

He wished he had a bench, so he could sit right next to Ines, and not have something between them. He planned to speak with the general store owners and see what could be made to fit that bill. Sunsets were enjoyable to watch with Ines, but he felt sure they would be even better with his arm around her shoulders.

He glanced over at her, and his heart tugged at seeing her face. Ines was worrying. Joseph reached over for her hand. "What are you thinking about?"

"The letter that arrived yesterday," she said softly.

"Ah."

The letter. His aunt's lawyer had been busy. Not only had he gone over every inch of the contract, he had also looked into Mr. Altrose and Hester.

Mr. Altrose had been cleared of all wrongdoing outside of being a little too loose with his tongue around Hester, when plied with fine food and drink. While many men might have that difficulty, Joseph felt that a man such as a lawyer ought to be more mindful. He'd be finding a new one soon.

As for Hester...well, as they'd suspected, Hester had a lot to do with Bess's sudden departure. Aunt Rosemary's lawyer had left no stone unturned, and had tracked Bess down. She admitted that she'd been paid a large sum of money by Hester to not marry Joseph, and it had made the choice between him and the hotel owner who'd asked for her hand easier.

Though Bess said she wouldn't come back, Joseph had the feeling that's what worried Ines.

"Joseph?"

"Hmm?" He looked over at her.

"Do you still want to marry me? Even knowing that I might not fully recover and be all the help you need on the ranch? I...I know there's not much time. But I was talking to Aunt Rosemary earlier." Ines stopped and took a deep breath. "She told me that she could get you another bride if you wanted one. There's something called a proxy marriage that could be done."

Joseph stared at her in shock. Finally, he said, "You know, a man could really start feeling poorly about himself, when all the women he tries to marry run off."

"I'm not trying to run off," Ines said heatedly. "I'm trying to let you have a choice. Some say. In something that you've not really had a say in." She was quiet then. "I understand. Forgive me. I know that the ranch is first and foremost on your mind, and you are worried if I leave, your chances of keeping it are slim. I—"

"Will you stop?" Joseph asked, frustrated. "Forget about the ranch for a minute."

Ines scowled at him. "I can't. That's the whole reason I was brought here." She crossed her arms over her chest.

"No," he argued. "That might have been it, at first. But the moment my aunt heard about my dilemma, she didn't just find me the first woman out there. She found me someone who was going to be good for me. Someone who I could love. Do love. She found me, as she told me all along, the person who I needed."

It was Joseph's turn to take a deep breath. "Now, I know you haven't gotten much say in this either. But, the fact of the matter is, you've not only surprised me, you've impressed me, the way you handle things out here and seem to fit in as though you've always been a part of my life. And, I like that," Joseph told her.

He crossed his arms over his chest. "Do you want to leave me?"

Chapter 18

"Do you want to leave me?" Joseph repeated. His voice was at a strange pitch, and he looked...nervous. His eyes were pleading with her, only, she wasn't sure what answer he wanted.

Ines blinked rapidly at him, unsure what to think or say or do. In the short time she'd known him, Joseph had always been so calm. Never really passionate or decisive about anything. That's why she never really knew where she stood with him. How he felt about, well, anything. This new side of him was...different.

Didn't he understand she didn't want to go? That she was doing this to give him a choice? To be kind? Not saddle him with a woman who might be weak and bedbound for who knows how long?

Ines felt…angry. Hurt. Scared. And she wasn't sure which of those emotions she should act on, and which she should shove into the smallest corners of her being, and barricade up so they didn't burst out and make her say something she'd regret. Because she didn't want to feel angry, not at Joseph. She cared for him. Was concerned about him keeping the ranch.

She was also disappointed. Joseph knew how she felt about him. Didn't he? Maybe she'd not been clear enough, but she was in love with him. And he…he didn't seem to return those feelings. At least, he'd not said so. When she first woke up, and he'd cupped her face, she had thought…

She was a fool. And that's why she was scared. Scared because here, once again, she'd let herself have just a little bit of hope, and, as usual, it was being taken away from her.

Tears started to form, but of what variety they were, Ines wasn't sure. She was exhausted. There was no other word for it. Exhausted of trying to be what everyone else wanted, all of the time, and make them happy. Now that it was time for her to say how she felt, she didn't know what to do. Say what she really wanted? Or say what she thought he wanted to hear?

"Ines." Joseph reached out and took her hand in his. "Look at me."

Though she didn't want to, didn't want him to see her face, her hurt and fear, Ines dragged her eyes toward

Joseph. He was looking at her with such kindness, such concern, it was about to be her undoing.

"Ines, listen to me. I don't really know how to say the things I'm thinking or feeling. I've never really had any practice, so I'm prepared to make a big mess of it all, but if I talk, will you listen?"

She nodded.

Joseph took a deep breath, and squeezed her hand gently. "All I want is you. Here. I don't want you to leave. I don't want another woman. I don't, most assuredly, want Bess."

He moved closer to her. "Ines, I am in love with you. I wasn't sure that's what I was feeling. At first, I tried to fight it. Hide it. Worried that you'd leave me, because this isn't an easy life. Not out here on a ranch. But, I think you love me. And I...I love you too."

Ines could hardly believe what he'd said. Her lips parted slightly in surprise, but she didn't speak, didn't want to interrupt him, in case she was dreaming. She didn't want to wake, if that was the case. No, she just wanted to hear his voice, his profession of love. The first she'd ever had in her life.

Joseph's voice caught, as he continued, "When I first saw you, after Hester attacked you, I was scared I'd lost you. That you wouldn't recover. Ines, I don't care if you have to spend the rest of your life in a chair. My life isn't worth anything at all if you aren't in it. If you need help,

I'll help you. Whatever you need, whatever you want. Just stay with me. Don't leave me.

"I know we've hardly known each other, but, once again, Aunt Rosemary is right. We are well suited. What you wanted, love, I want that too. And if you'd just let me try, let me try to be the man I want to be for you, I think we can have that together.

"And," he went on, "if the ranch is too much, I'll sell it. Move away. Go wherever you want. Even if it's back to California. Because I want to make you happy. That's all I want. To see you happy and content. I'll go anywhere, as long as I get to be with you."

Ines couldn't stop the smile from filling her face. Her heart felt so light. So happy. "Do you really mean that?" she asked in a whisper.

"I do. But I know you have doubts. Is it about me? About how I say I will love you?" he asked.

Ines thought for a moment, then answered, "I guess...perhaps I'm not sure I can be all a man wants. What you want. Especially if later we find out something's wrong in my head, after I was struck. I don't want to be what isn't good enough for you."

"Ines," he said quietly, kneeling before her and taking her hands in his. "You can't be what every man wants, just like I can't be what every woman wants. But you are *just* what I want. And I hope at least part of me is what you want. I don't want to think about things that might not be. I know you'll fully recover, I have faith in that, but if you don't, I'll be by your side, loving you, taking care of you, protecting you."

Ines didn't know what to say. Her heart was pounding and her stomach was queasy. She wasn't expecting that to happen.

"Will you stay?" Joseph asked. "Will you marry me?"

Chapter 19

Ines reached out and let one of her hands rest on Joseph's cheek. It was slightly rough and tickled her palm. The hopeful look in his eyes warmed her whole body. To think, he really did love her. Was willing to even give up his ranch for her!

With a gasp, Ines dropped her hand. "Oh no!" she said.

"What? What?" Joseph asked, looking around. "What do you see? Hester?" the word was spoken in a growl.

"No, no, not him," Ines reassured, grabbing his hands. "It's just, I can't let you sell the ranch. Not for me."

"Don't you understand I would? That your happiness means more to me than anything else?" Joseph asked.

She smiled, and stepped indecently close to him. "I don't want you to, though," she told him. "I love the ranch. And I love you. And...and I want to marry you and stay here."

Her chest felt like it was nearly squeezing, as she waited for Joseph's reply. But it came in a very unexpected way.

Before Ines could blink, he had leaned down and brushed his lips against hers. Her entire body tingled, and her head felt light. A dizzying sensation filled her, and as he moved back, Ines put her fingertips to her lips.

She was sure she was red faced. That had been...wonderful. It had also been her first kiss, and she hoped that she had done it correctly. Shyly, she glanced up at Joseph, who was grinning down at her.

Ines thought that Joseph was about to kiss her again, when the door opened and Aunt Rosemary came out of the house.

"It's about time!" she said. "Goodness. I was starting to get concerned that my success rate was going to drop. And not a moment too soon. I've simply got to go back home."

She went to Ines, and looked at her pleadingly. "You understand, don't you, dear? The air is so dry! It simply won't do for my skin. The dust...it gets everywhere. I'll never be able to wash it all away. Plus, there are others who need me."

"I do understand," Ines assured her. She wrapped her arms around Aunt Rosemary, much to the other woman's surprise. "Thank you," Ines whispered, her voice catching. "Thank you for finding me Joseph."

Joseph joined her in wrapping an arm around his aunt. "Yes, thank you, Aunt Rosemary. I don't even have the words for it."

"Of course you don't," his aunt sniffed, as she stepped back and smoothed her dress. "One simply cannot comprehend nor verbalize the level of intense scrutiny and degree of difficulty that I endure, going through my books to match others."

"It's a real talent," Ines said, smiling at her.

"One must do what one does best," Aunt Rosemary agreed. Then she studied Ines. "Are you up for trying on your dress? After all, you've a wedding to prepare for."

"I am," Ines agreed.

Joseph's aunt fixed him in a glare. "And you! You had better be dressed appropriately."

"I will be," he promised with a grin. "Only the best for my bride to be."

Aunt Rosemary made a sound of satisfaction, and led Ines to the house. Ines glanced over her shoulder and smiled at Joseph. What a colossal mistake she had almost made. She had been so willing to give up her chance at love, because she thought that he didn't really want her, that she'd almost missed out on Joseph, and his love.

As Ines stood before a mirror in the lovely new dress she planned to wear for her wedding, Aunt Rosemary fussing and tugging and making little sounds as she looked this way and that, Ines couldn't help but wonder how many moments in her life would have been so different, if she'd just been truthful about what she wanted.

When Aunt Rosemary stepped back, a pleased expression on her face, and pronounced Ines perfect, Ines ventured, "May I ask you a question? It might be personal in nature."

"Well," the older woman said thoughtfully, "you did save my life, so I suppose I can at least hear the question. I don't promise an answer, though."

"It's just..." Ines tried to figure out how to word what was on her mind. "I want to be more like you. Speak my mind. Make my own happiness. I realize that I waited too long. Wasted too many years, always doing what others expected of me, letting their happiness always overshadow my own. How do I...how do I be more like you?"

Aunt Rosemary turned toward the window and rested a hand on the sill as she looked out it. "For a long time," she finally said, "I lived my life as you did. Perhaps for too long. It makes me happy to see you, at a far younger age than I was, able to fight for some of the happiness that you deserve."

Ines moved next to the older woman. "I had no idea. I guess I thought that everything was always...I don't know."

"Perfect for me? For everyone but you?" Aunt Rosemary asked, her lips twitching into a smile. "It seems that way, sometimes, doesn't it? But remember, my dear, that it's not. We all have difficulties, and we all have things we don't wish others to see. Some are better at hiding it than others."

Ines was quiet for a moment. Sorrow for the older woman, and something akin to worry, filled her. She met the other woman's eyes, and whispered, "Are you happy now?"

Aunt Rosemary smiled. It wasn't one of her tightlipped, proper smiles. It was filled with warmth and love. "Yes, dear girl," she said. "Because now, I get to make sure that so many others have what I didn't have for so long."

She sucked in a deep breath. "Goodness. The wind outside seems to have loosened my tongue more than I meant. No more questions."

Ines nodded, and they stood there quietly together, looking through the window at nothing at all, lost in their separate thoughts.

Later that night, as she lay in bed, Ines sent a prayer heavenward, that Aunt Rosemary would one day have the opportunity to have some of the love that she had helped assure for others.

Her last thought, as a yawn escaped and her heavy eyes closed, was that in just a matter of hours, she'd be married, and receive another one of those lovely kisses from Joseph.

Chapter 20

Joseph stood at the stagecoach office window. When it was his turn, he approached the window. "One ticket, please," he said, tapping on the map where he wanted the stage to go.

"That'll be six dollars," the man behind the counter said.

He slid the money over, accepted the ticket, and turned back to where his aunt was waiting, Ines by her side and luggage at her feet.

"We'll miss you," Ines was saying tearfully as he walked closer.

"We will write," his aunt said, taking Ines's hand. "Now, back straight. Smile on your lips. A lady never acts emotional in public. And, Joseph," his aunt said, turning to him.

"Ma'am?" he asked, straightening his back.

"Much better. Slouching doesn't show confidence in oneself," she told him. Likely for the fiftieth time since she'd arrived.

"Stage coming!" someone called out.

Aunt Rosemary's face twisted into an expression of distaste, before she threw back her shoulders and smoothed her features. "Thank goodness. It's time to leave this dusty town. Ines, I'll give your parents your love. Joseph, please see they handle my bags with care."

His aunt smiled then, and clapped her hands together once. "I cannot wait to get back home and tell everyone about my successful match. It gives hope to so many," she added, shaking her head with a look of sorrow. "So many seek love; so few find it. But once again, I've done my part, and to help in this barren wasteland, no less."

Not exactly sure what he should say to that, Joseph approached the stage, both to ensure his aunt's bags were loaded, and to warn the driver he was about to have a fastidious passenger.

His aunt and Ines approached a moment later, Cal helping with the bags, handing them over to be secured.

"Safe travels," Ines said, kissing his aunt's cheek and grasping her hands. "Thank you for all you've done for me."

"Bags are all safe and sound, Miss Rosemary," Cal said with a wink at his aunt.

To Joseph's surprise, his aunt flushed slightly. "Thank you," she said, moving toward the stage.

"Reckon if I wrote you, you'd write me back?" Cal asked, clutching his hat in his hands.

Joseph was sure his jaw had dropped. Ines's eyes were wide as they stared between the two.

"Perhaps," was his aunt's reply. "I suppose you'll just have to find out."

The stage door closed, and the driver cracked the whip. The stage flew away, and Joseph waved, glancing over to see Ines doing the same. Cal had disappeared.

Ines looked at him and giggled. "I never imagined I'd hear that."

"You and me both," Joseph said. "Do you really think she will write him if he writes her?"

Ines wrapped her arm around his, and they slowly walked back toward their wagon. "I don't know. Maybe. She told me a lot of stories while I was in bed for so long. I think...I think part of the reason your aunt loves to make matches for others isn't just because she's good at it, but she really does want others to find love. It may not always work out, but she does try. And I think she deserves that for herself."

"I do too," Joseph agreed. "And she sure did good, putting us together."

"Yes, she did." Ines smiled, and let him help her into the wagon seat. "Should we wait for Cal?" she asked, twisting to look for the foreman. "I know he rode his horse, but we did all come together."

"Nah, he knows the way back," Joseph said. "Not to mention, this is the first time we've had to be alone, just us. Let's enjoy the quiet."

It was true. Right after their wedding yesterday, where Ines had stood before him in the prettiest dress he'd ever seen, there had been a potluck supper, and just about everyone had wanted to talk to the two of them.

Joseph had only wanted a small church wedding, but word had gotten around, and it had grown to near half the town. By the time they got home, both he and Ines were half asleep. Even Aunt Rosemary had dozed off in the wagon on the ride back.

"I know your aunt thinks this a barren wasteland," Ines said, turning her face up to the sky, "but I love it here. The fresh air, the beautiful mountains and wildflowers. Oregon has all I want. All I could ever want."

"Really?" Joseph asked, slightly surprised. "I know you say that, but I still wonder if you'll be happy without all the entertainment you surely had at home."

"What's more entertaining than watching you and Storm play catch? Watching the clouds roll across the sky, seeing the snowcapped mountains, soaking in the sunshine, and picking more wildflowers than I could possibly learn the names of? Not to mention picnics by the stream, rides around the ranch." Ines shrugged. "I meant it. All I want is here. And, in case you didn't realize, what I was also saying is all I want is you."

"I was hoping that's what you meant," Joseph said, wrapping his arm around her. "Because I can't think of anything I want more than I want you."

As they rode back to the ranch—their ranch—with Ines's head on his shoulder, Joseph said a silent thank you to his father. Things had not gone as he'd once thought they would, and there had been some heartache along the way, but he wouldn't have traded any of that, since it brought him Ines.

He'd meant every word he'd told her when he was near begging for her to stay. The ranch didn't mean anything to him if he didn't have her by his side. Though he wished his parents were around to be able to see him happy with Ines, and fall in love with her as much as he had, he had the feeling they were watching over them.

The wagon pulled up to the house, and Storm came out, wagging her tail and barking a greeting. Joseph swung Ines down from the wagon, but held her tightly in his arms. As she rested her head against his chest, he marveled at how well she fit there.

Though she was gone, his aunt's voice drifted through his mind, as the memory of the first moment he'd seen Ines played through his head.

"Joseph, this is Ines Martin," Aunt Rosemary had said, making introductions. "I think you will find she is just what you need, and I have brought her to be your wife."

How right his aunt had been, in every way. Why had he doubted her for even a second?

Joseph squeezed Ines gently, and then released her, taking her hand and leading her to the porch. He nodded a thanks to one of the ranch hands as they led the wagon away. "You are just what I need," he said, sitting next to her in one of the rocking chairs. "I promise never to make you doubt that."

Ines didn't answer, just gave him that sweet smile of hers that had captured his heart far sooner than he'd have ever admitted. They sat, taking in the cattle and horses roaming in the distance, and throwing sticks for Storm to chase.

They were still sitting there, an hour later, when Cal rode up, grinning at them. "Sent me a letter!" he called out. "Might be me getting a bride one day."

Ines laughed, and the sound filled Joseph's heart with happiness. Joseph felt like the luckiest man alive. A far, far different feeling from when he'd written to his aunt as his last resort.

Epilogue

Four months later

"You've a letter," Joseph said, reaching into his pocket. "Cal just brought it from town."

"Oh! From my parents," Ines said, looking at it. She wiped her hands off on her apron and sat at the kitchen table to open it.

"Anything important?" Joseph asked.

"My sister returned home," Ines said. "It appears that her marriage didn't work out. I have the feeling my sister will never hear the end of it."

"Maybe Aunt Rosemary can find her someone," Joseph said, reaching into the cookie jar and removing a handful of oatmeal cookies.

"She had before. Only, my sister didn't want him." Ines shrugged. "She'll have to figure that out on her own.

My parents also say that they are hoping to visit for Christmas."

"That sounds nice," Joseph said. "I'm looking forward to meeting them."

"Do you think there will be too much snow for them to get here?" Ines asked.

Joseph chewed a bite, thinking for a moment. "Write and tell them to leave a little earlier than they think. The train can likely make it. It's the stage they'd have to be concerned about. Until we get rail tracks out this way, it's going to be a little more difficult."

"I'll do that now," Ines said. "Christmas is only two months away! Do you think your aunt might like an invitation?"

"You can send her one," Joseph said, "but if I know my aunt, she'll be busy with holiday parties, and filling her books with names and information about others."

Ines laughed, but didn't disagree. Joseph was likely right. Still, she would write to her as well, and see if she wanted to join her parents.

Joseph leaned over and kissed her cheek, then moved to the back door. "I'm going to be in the south pasture," he told her. "Ring the porch bell if you need me."

"I will," Ines said. She put the kettle on, and got some paper and her pencil. As her tea steeped, she started to write her letters.

She was looking forward to Christmas with her family, and hoped her sister would come. Though they'd had their disagreements in the past, she didn't want her sister to be sad or lonely. Perhaps Aunt Rosemary could help. One thing she'd learned is you were never too old for love, and you were never unworthy of it.

Just then, Joseph rushed back into the kitchen, and Ines looked at him in surprise. "Did you forget something?" she asked.

"I did," he said, and leaned over to give her another kiss. "I forgot to tell you I love you, Ines. And I'll love you every day for the rest of my life. I just wanted you to know that."

He was gone before she could answer, and Ines brought her fingers to her lips to touch where he'd just brushed his against hers.

Even though she knew he couldn't hear her, she whispered, "I love you too, Joseph. And I always will."

Note from Author

Thank you for taking the time to read *Joseph's Last Resort*.
Could I ask for one small favor? Reviews like yours on
Amazon mean so much to me and help others to find my
books! Even just a single line means a lot!

Also...

Want a FREE book?

Stop by my website to get your no strings attached **FREE
book**. It's my gift to you, as a thank you for reading this
one.

www.sarahlambbooks.com

Want all of the Aunt Rosemary books?

Romancing the Wrangler

Rose and Levi only have one rule—make their own rules.

Free spirited Rose Alden is her father's youngest child, and his disappointment. Her sharp mind and wit are matched only by her sarcastic tongue and disobedience in finding a suitable husband like her older sisters did. She's desperate to live her own life, make her own rules, and marriage is not something she is interested in.

Ranch hand Levi Patterson understands just how Rose feels. It's why he's grateful to be working for her father on the Alden's quiet ranch. However, the past he thought he'd left behind has caught up, demanding he choose between the needs of others and his own.

A sudden change of events forces them each to make a decision that will change the future forever. Will Rose fight for what she longs for? Can Levi return to what was, or will he continue to blaze his own path with Rose by his side?

https://www.amazon.com/Romancing-Wrangler-Second-Chance-Groom-ebook/dp/B0CFWJB2W4/

***

Millie's Wedding Dilemma

When Millie Hudson is introduced to Dr. Winston Felton, it's love at first sight. She can hardly wait to become his wife and eagerly makes plans for their new life together. However, days before their wedding, her new mother-in-law, Mother Nola, announces she's moving in. And everything changes.

Dr. Winston Felton is overjoyed Millie is his new bride. She's everything and more that he dreamed of in a woman, and his patients adore her. She's even tolerant and sweet to his overbearing mother and tries hard to form a bond with her. No small task, considering his mother will never let any of them forget Millie was not *her* pick for him.

As if navigating a new marriage and her mother-in-law weren't enough, a strange man starts lurking around.

Millie is terrified Mother Nola, being a wealthy widow, might be the victim of a blackmailer. Though she's been treated unkindly, Millie is determined to protect her, at any cost.

However, the truth is far more shocking than she could have imagined—and comes at a cost none of them foresaw.

https://www.amazon.com/Millies-Wedding-Dilemma-Mother-Law-ebook/dp/B0CQ9XTZG9

About the Author

Sarah writes captivating characters and clean romance that's anything BUT boring! From heartbreaking moments to heartwarming tales, get swept away in either historical or small town romance that pulls you in until the last page.

Nestled in the Blue Ridge Mountains of Virginia where she's married to her Texan husband, you'll find Sarah creating her next book, homeschooling her two boys, or volunteering in her community.

Want more of Sarah's books? Find them all on Amazon!

https://www.amazon.com/stores/Sarah-Lamb/auth
or/B098H3SGLK